WISH UPON A SATELLITE

SOPHIE LABELLE

Second Story Press

Library and Archives Canada Cataloguing in Publication

Title: Wish upon a satellite / Sophie Labelle.
Names: Labelle, Sophie, 1988- author.
Identifiers: Canadiana (print) 20210307722 | Canadiana (ebook)
    20210307730 | ISBN 9781772602579 (softcover) | ISBN
    9781772602586 (EPUB)
Classification: LCC PS8623.A23235 W57 2022 | DDC jC813/.6—dc23

Cover by Sophie Labelle

Printed and bound in Canada

*Second Story Press gratefully acknowledges the support of the
Ontario Arts Council and the Canada Council for the Arts for our
publishing program. We acknowledge the financial support of the
Government of Canada through the Canada Book Fund.*

ONTARIO ARTS COUNCIL
CONSEIL DES ARTS DE L'ONTARIO

Canada Council   Conseil des Arts
for the Arts   du Canada

Funded by the Government of Canada
Financé par le gouvernement du Canada | 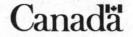 Canadä

Published by
SECOND STORY PRESS
20 Maud Street, Suite 401
Toronto, ON M5V 2M5
www.secondstorypress.ca

MIX
Paper from
responsible sources
FSC
www.fsc.org   FSC® C016245

Wish Upon a Satellite

WISH UPON
A
SATELLITE

CHAPTER 1

STEPHANIE BONDU'S LIPS are everything you would think they are: they make you feel at home and they taste like honeydew lip balm. I had no clue I needed these lips in my life so much, until now.

It's because, you see, Stephanie Bondu has been my best friend since fifth grade. We've had countless sleepovers before tonight. She was there for me during my first heartbreak, and I was there for her that time she scored less than 90% on an exam. So, you know, I should have known about these lips. They were right under my nose. Well, under her nose, technically.

It's probably too much info, but we spent about ten minutes exchanging saliva and snot during the most intense smooching session of my life. That's longer than my ex-boyfriend and I ever did. Everything I experienced before feels kind of fake now.

And it happened just like that. No warning signs, no anticipation. Well, okay, we were hugging, but that's what you would expect from BFFs when one of them just dumped her terrible boyfriend for the fifteenth time. She sent me a text message shortly after dinner saying that, this time, it really was over with Frank. She seemed really pissed. So, I gulped the *bolo de rolo* cake my dad made for my little brother (it's his favorite, my dad's way of apologizing for leaving him at home tomorrow while we go on our last cycling trip before winter) and went to meet Stephie at her mom's.

It started with a long rant about Frank, whom she's been dating since time immemorial. Turns out this bad excuse for a boyfriend asked Stephie for nudes because his best friend Viktor got some from his girlfriend. Now, I don't really know that girlfriend. I mean, I know her face and I can remember her name (it's Raquel) because we went to the same elementary school, but that's pretty much it. She's been quite rude to Stephie and me in the past. If she wants to do something as questionable and potentially illegal as sending nude pictures of her underage self to the smelly, thoroughly average soccer player that is Viktor, I guess that's her choice. But I draw the line at these boys thinking they can ask for them.

As Stephie was telling me everything, I was angry. First, at Stephie's pain: it was so unfair to her! Frank should have known that she has body image issues. Feeling validated in her body shouldn't come at a price. It hits her where she is most vulnerable. And if she wasn't so opinionated, she might have fallen for it—letting Frank play with her self-esteem in such a toxic way.

Second…how the heck did Frank know about Raquel's nudes? Did Viktor share them around? Apparently, when Stephie confronted Frank about it, he simply said that it's what boys talk about in locker rooms. Stephie didn't buy it. If she had sent him any pictures, Frank could have used them to brag to his soccer teammates and showed them around, which is probably what happened with Raquel's.

She broke down while she was telling me the story, her anger giving way to despair. She had to stop talking because her sobbing hiccups made it too hard. As we were both hugging on her new bed (she outgrew her princessy, four-poster one), I instinctively pulled her closer and patted her hair. And I guess it worked? She calmed herself and we ended up cuddling, like many times before, although it never culminated in something as intimate as the hot mess we're in right now.

The tears stopped. We spent an eternity resting our heads on her pillows, staring into each other's eyes. Strands of hair dried onto her cheeks. Every boiling emotion turned into body heat that felt familiar. I had no clue what just happened. All I know is that it was real. I must look like a deer in the headlights. What's the expression in her tired, bloodshot eyes? Maybe it's just drowsiness. I can't really tell.

We're holding hands. I wish we could kiss again, I could use some of that honeydew lip balm. But her eyes are now closed, and I wouldn't dare. So, I just press my forehead against hers to feel her breath near my mouth. Soon, she's asleep. Too many things are going through my mind for me to go to sleep.

This is the first time I've kissed a girl, and it was great. Does that mean I'm bisexual? I know Stephie is, but I never really thought about it myself. Not that I care, particularly. I don't feel like either a boy or a girl. It makes every potential relationship kind of gay.

Will it change our friendship? Can we still go see bad movies together and ship every character in the most bizarre ways possible? Above her ponytail, which is draped lazily around her neck, her *Lafontaine* poster is on her wall, that musical we're both huge fans of. We're supposed to go see it in November. My dad bought us tickets last year for my birthday, and we've been waiting impatiently ever since. Does that mean we'll go as a date? That we'll both need to dress fancy to impress each other during a romantic pre-show dinner, instead of nerding out with all our *Lafontaine* gear while stuffing ourselves with piles of greasy poutine?

I gently reach in the pocket of my dress to grab my phone with my free hand. I have a notification from Liam, the person I trust the most after Stephie and my dog Borki. We're weirdly close, considering I only met him last year. He's a shy and awkward nerd, although you probably wouldn't expect such a manga fanatic to also be an international-level athlete. His wall is decorated with medals and trophies he's won during swimming competitions—along with tons of Japanese-style art he makes. He's a guy of many talents.

I told Liam I was spending the evening with Stephie because shit hit the fan with Frank.

Hey Ciel! Everything alright?

Even though it's not my legal name, my close friends call me Ciel. It means "sky" in French. It feels more colorful, changing, and evocative than "Alex," the name I'm called at school.

Yeah. She cried a lot. She's asleep now.

That bad, eh?

You have no idea. Frank has been such a jerk.

What happened?

I type several attempts at explaining the whole story, but nothing feels right. I just say,

I'll tell you at school, it's complicated.

Oh. Okay.

How's the competition?

Liam's spending the weekend on the other side of the border, near New York City, to splash around with the other North Americans. At this point, it's not even special for him anymore.

It's fine. I made it to the finals tomorrow. Saw some guys I knew from New England.

Sweet.

He sends a picture of a hamburger and a milkshake on what seems to be a hotel bed.

My teammates and I are having room service dinner!

Ooh, fancy!

I put my phone on selfie mode and send him a portrait of myself putting my tongue out. My hair is all over Stephie's pillow.

Ooh, sexy!

I'm the dessert.

Of course.

We often pretend to flirt, but it's just a game. I know he's not interested in going out with me: he told me when I asked him a while ago. He said he's not ready to be that close to anyone, or something like that. I still think we'd make a good couple.

Stephie is snoring beside me. I'm itching to tell Liam about our kiss. It's all I can focus on. But I don't know, it would feel weird to tell that kind of stuff to a boy I had a crush on. What if he thinks I'm only telling him to make him jealous or something? But I have to tell someone. And I'm sure I'll end up telling him anyway. He is one of my best friends, after all.

Also, I guess Stephie and I are smooching buddies, now? Idk.

Oh! That was unexpected.

Same.

So, she made the first move? She's such a Capricorn. You have to tell me more!

I can call you tomorrow evening, after my cycling trip?

We'll see. I think we arrive in Montréal at 9 pm. The time to get our bags, take the airport shuttle to the subway, and the subway home, it's gonna be pretty late....

Fine. Well, enjoy your milkshake with this new layer of suspense in it, then!

Slurp slurp!

★ ★ ★

It's about 10 p.m. when Stephie wakes up. She wipes her eyes and asks, "Did I sleep?"

I put my phone down. I've been playing games on it for at least an hour. I bend over Stephie, look at her in disbelief, and put my hands on her shoulders. "Stephie!! You've been asleep for TWO WHOLE YEARS!"

"Ha ha ha! Is that why you're wearing the same clothes as when I last saw you?"

"Just a coincidence."

She reaches to get her own phone from the charger on the little table near her bed. Her expression changes as she scrolls through her notifications.

"You missed a couple of calls. I figured I'd let you sleep instead."

"I'm glad you did."

She puts her phone back on the table and sighs. No need to ask who's been calling her. She passes one hand through her hair to smooth the strands tangled by dried tears and looks at me.

"Do you want to sleep here?"

"I'd love to, but we're leaving early tomorrow morning."

"Right, you're going on your cycling trip."

"My dad and I, yeah. We're going to the West Island, then to Vaudreuil, and then to see the Beauharnois locks."

"I have no clue where any of these places are."

"You know the West Island, at least? The western part of Montréal. We're in the East, now. If you go to the western-most end of the island, you get to the Saint Lawrence river. Vaudreuil is on the other side of it. Last time we went, it was very pretty."

"Noice. Send me pictures."

"Of course!"

Stephie lies down and puts my hand on her head.

"Wanna cuddle some more?"

★ ★ ★

I don't put the brakes on when I'm cycling down Rosemont Boulevard in the fresh October night air, and it feels like I'm flying. The neighborhood where Stephie and I live is in the easternmost point of the plateau stretching out from Mount Royal, the mountain that gives its name to the city it overlooks. It gets hilly in places, but it's not much compared to the Visitation slope, which we need to climb in order to reach our neighborhood from the downtown area. Fortunately, I really only climb it when I go to the youth meeting at the LGBT+ Center.

The streets are usually empty, except for some folks getting last-minute snacks and drinks from the dépanneur, a French Canadian corner store, and a couple of suspicious tomcats minding their own business. Sometimes, if you're lucky, you can also see one of the foxes who live in the nearby Maisonneuve Park. They like to visit when the city is quiet. There are also bunnies; it's a huge park, but we rarely see them in the streets.

As I unlock the door, I notice that the living room light is on. My dad is still up.

"Hey, sweetie. How was your evening?"

Borki yaps before coming to lick my leg. I scratch his little head and say, not too loud since my brother is probably sleeping, "Good boy! It was intense. Stephie is really upset at Frank. He asked her for nude pictures, can you imagine?"

"Nude pictures of who?"

"Of herself. Frank's friend got some from his girlfriend, so...."

"Oh dear."

"Yeah. So, you understand...."

"Precisely."

I look at my dad, sitting between piles of exams scattered around him. It was mid-semester in colleges last week, so we haven't seen the color of the couch since then. He teaches chemistry in the North of the city. "Anything else?"

"Nah, I should go to bed now."

"You still want to leave at seven tomorrow?"

"I'm so ready for it!"

"Alright. First up wakes the other one! How about dropping by a Tim Hortons for breakfast on the road?"

"Aww, yes!"

CHAPTER 2

MY DAD AND I cross the river at the height of the Deux-Montagnes Lake, below two mountains that look like a pair of butt cheeks, to hop from Montréal Island to Perrot Island to the mainland to Valleyfield Island, where the dam and the Beauharnois locks are located—our first rest stop. As we planned, we arrive there at around 1 p.m., right on time for lunch. My dad and I are experts at this.

We unpack our food on a picnic table in the park near the huge locks. Cargo boats from the Great Lakes use them to avoid the Saint Lawrence dam, their last big obstacle before the ocean. My mom used to take us here, my brother and me, to look at the boats going up and down from one lock to another. Which is why I chose this place for our last cycling trip of the year.

I read on one of the boats, "Mil-wau-kee…? Where's that, again?"

"In Wisconsin, near Chicago. It's by Lake Michigan."

Some of these boats are coming from pretty far away and going even further. Detroit, Toronto, Rochester, Chicago… they all have to stop here before going to China or New Zealand, or wherever they feel like. It always fascinated me how this small stream could open up the rest of the world to an entire continent.

Before we eat, I take a picture of the cargo ship from Milwaukee to send it to Stephie and Liam, along with a message that I'm still alive. I didn't update them on our journey yet, since Stephie is probably still asleep, and Liam had his competition this morning. I figured he might be busy. Liam replies instantly:

A boat?? I thought you were cycling today!

Oh, you.

He sends me a picture of the pool from his seat. There must be a hundred boys in swimsuits going around, and I can't resist joking about it.

Nice view!

I know, right? Such lovely sights. Gotta go now! It'll be my turn in half an hour.

You got this!

Thanks! Have a nice ride.

When I put my phone down, my dad is done arranging our picnic on the table. He looks at me. "What's that grin on your face?"

"It's Liam, he's at a swimming competition in New York."

"I hope he's doing well."

"Can't be better, surrounded by all those cute boys."

"I see. That's what's happening."

I smile at my dad, who looks back at me with suspicion in his eyes. He knows that I asked Liam out and that he said no, and now he probably wonders if joking about cute boys with him makes me feel better. He probably knows it doesn't. He probably wants me to tell him I'm fine.

I take a bite of my veggie wrap after dipping it in garlic hummus.

"I think I might be bisexual."

My dad's eyes go wide. He wasn't prepared for that. I mean, he doesn't look surprised, just…unprepared. How can anything surprise him? My parents thought I was gay since I was a toddler. I've been verbalizing the fact that I wasn't really a boy most of my life. I told him I was in love with a boy in my class when I was seven. And I managed to pass French with an average of 64%, last year. So, nothing can really surprise him anymore.

He starts eating his chicken wrap.

"Is that what's been on your mind today?"

"Kinda…?"

"I was worried you were going through a heartbreak."

I laugh.

"No, not at all. I think it's the opposite of a heartbreak."

"Oh, really? Someone I know?"

I take a sip from my box of soy milk.

"Well, yesterday, when I went to Stephie's place, we kind of…kissed?"

My dad raises a very high eyebrow. He stops chewing for a short moment. Now, that's the face he makes when he's genuinely surprised.

"Oh."

"Yeah."

"So that's serious?"

"I'm not sure. I don't know. It was confusing. We haven't really talked about it since. She fell asleep. But it was nice."

My dad takes another bite and touches the bridge of his nose. Something's bothering him. The silence makes me uncomfortable. I continue, "It's not like we're a couple now. We were cuddling and it happened. I wouldn't mind it happening again, that's all I'm saying."

"You have to be careful with these things. You have a precious and rare friendship with Stephie. And you told me she just broke up with her boyfriend."

"Frank? Yeah, for like the twentieth time."

"It sounds like she was struggling. Maybe it's a bit rushed?"

"Dad, we're not getting married. We were just cuddling, and, and…. I shouldn't have told you about this."

14

"I'm sorry, Alex. I'm just worried about you."

"I'll be fine."

I don't say anything else and concentrate on my food. When my dad calls me "Alex," I know he's being serious. I attempt to change the subject.

"So, we're getting on the maritime cycling path now?"

"Not quite yet. There's another three or four hours to cycle before we get there."

"Oh, that's right. I remember. We need to go through Kahnawake."

"That's what we did last time, but I think it would actually be quicker if we went through the fields, instead. Here…."

He takes out a map from one of the bags. We both have phones with map apps, but my dad always carries paper ones. I find it a bit silly and more complicated, but it's part of the tradition. Also, it's hilarious to watch him struggle to fold it back in place each time.

"See this road? It takes us to Châteauguay, and this is the road to Kahnawake, the Mohawk town. But if we cut here and follow the Châteauguay river for a bit…. Did you know there are two towns named 'Châteauguay' near here? One at the source of the river, in upstate New York, and one at the mouth of it, over there, facing Montréal's West Island."

"Ha ha. 'Châteauguay.' Gay castle."

"That's definitely the funniest part of what I just said."

"I know!"

"Anyway, we follow the river for a bit. We pass Highway 30. We get to a cycling path that takes us through some fields, all the way to the maritime cycling path, right there, in Sainte-Catherine."

"Sweet. Let's do that."

★ ★ ★

If it were summer, it would have been painful to spend the day cycling under the sun. But, luckily for us, the air is fresh and the colder temperature helps with the intense sun.

It's almost 4 p.m. when we reach the maritime cycling path. It used to be just a narrow string of rocks in the Saint Lawrence River that created a clear channel for boats to navigate past the rapids near Montréal. It was repurposed into a cycling path decades ago, or so my dad told me.

Both sides of the cycling path are covered in trees and bushes, and the waves of the Saint Lawrence crash against them. And right now, in the midst of fall, most of the maple trees have already turned red. I keep asking my dad to stop so I can take pictures.

"See the bridge over there? That's where we cross back to Montréal's island. At the end of the maritime cycling path, we'll end up on Notre Dame Island, where we could take a break before the last stretch back home. Sounds good?"

Once we get there and find a spot to settle down for a bit, I send my favorite picture of the fiery maples to Stephie and Liam. While we were cycling, Stephie finally got up and heart-reacted the boat picture I'd sent her. When she sees the new one, she writes:

Wow! Almost makes me want to go outside. Almost.

You should! It's so pretty right now.

Just like you!

I feel my cheeks turning red. It's silly because we always say that kind of shit to each other. I'm not sure if she's flirting with me or simply being my BFF. Because every time one of us says something that could describe someone, the other says, "just like you." Like, if someone casually mentions, "This sword has been forged by gods in the blood of a hundred mortals," the other says, "just like you," and it's like a free compliment and a nice figure of speech. Very poetic. Then you say, "Awww!" and the other winks. So I go,

Awww!

And she writes,

;)

I hesitate before writing anything else. I have no clue where Stephie wants to take this. So, I inquire,

How are you feeling?

Burnt. I don't want to do anything today.

Not even the book report Ms. Campeau gave us last Friday?

That doesn't count. That's fun.

I can't help but make a squinty face. No way my dyslexic ass would get any fun out of reading a novel for the sake of writing a report about it. The dancing ellipsis appears, and Stephie sends me a new message.

Thanks again for coming to my rescue last night.
You're the bestest.

Anytime! <3

<3

I must be smiling way too big because my dad notices. He laughs and says, "Focus! Eat your snack. I want to be home by seven-thirty at the latest."

"Are we getting delivery for dinner?"

"You bet. I'm pooped."

"Virgil could cook for us!"

"We would end up with cereal for dinner. I've learned my lesson."

We both laugh, thinking about the last time Virgil cooked. He managed to mess up spaghetti so badly that we couldn't even finish our plates.

I pick some granola bars and an apple out of the bag. My dad continues, "Did I ever tell you about how they made this island we're on?"

"What do you mean? It's not a real island?"

"Well, it's a real island, I assure you you're not dreaming it, but it's human-made. When they built Montréal's subway, for Expo '67, all the earth they excavated from the ground was transported by trucks and dumped here, in the middle of the river."

I look all around me. I have trouble believing I would have been sitting in the middle of the river some fifty years ago.

"That was part of the exposition. Montréalers wanted to show all the feats they could accomplish."

"That's silly. There's already tons of islands around here."

"I'm just telling you. This island wasn't there, and now it is."

"It doesn't make any sense."

"I know!"

I finish eating, thinking about dams and flooded areas and artificial islands and the big bridge I'm about to cross. Before we leave, my phone vibrates. It's a notification from my Discord app, "Liam Johnson sent you a picture." I unlock the screen: it's a selfie of Liam with a police officer. Except that the police officer looks particularly annoyed, which contrasts with Liam's big smile and cheery eyes.

Did you get in trouble??

You have no idea, mate. The entire NYPD probably hates me now.

What happened??

Hahaha! Can't explain right now. I'm safe, I'm already at the airport.

WTF Liam.

Hahaha

How did the tournament go?

Meh. Not too bad. We qualified for finals, and one of my teammates got 8th place. I didn't make it to the leaderboard tho.

That's too bad.

I really have to go now, we're taking off and my phone is already supposed to be on airplane mode. Hope you're having fun! Byyyyye

★ ★ ★

Once we have passed the gigantic, green Jacques Cartier Bridge, we cycle on Papineau Avenue until we reach the Visitation slope. My dad is completely exhausted and he needs to walk his bicycle up, but I manage to find some scraps of energy in my calves and work my way to the top from where we can see Lafontaine Park.

This time, I actually know a bit of history about that park; it's named after Louis-Hippolyte Lafontaine, the first French-speaking Canadian prime minister whose life story inspired Stephie's and my favorite musical, *Lafontaine*. Simply looking at the trees and the shape of the huge pond, a couple blocks away, reminds me of that vision I had the other night of Stephie and me going to see the show next month as a couple. Maybe I'd wear some kind of dapper outfit. Stephie has a thing for suits. And we'd go to a restaurant beforehand. That'd be nice. But then, any situation would be nice. Stephie is great. Also, I should ask her to let me see her book report when she's done with it, so I can get some inspiration for mine. I should also probably read the book.

My dad finally joins me at the top of the slope. He tries to catch his breath. In his defense, he's carrying most of our stuff, including food, water, changes of clothes, tools, maps, first aid kit, bear spray (better safe than sorry), and emergency tubes, so his bike must be heavier than mine.

"We're about twenty minutes away from home. Give me a minute, I'll send a message to your brother to meet us there."

Virgil spent the day with João, his best friend. He's probably the reason why my brother speaks much better Portuguese than I do; unlike us, João was born in Brazil and his family only arrived in Montréal when he was five. In kindergarten, he didn't speak a word of French, so my brother started helping him since my dad often speaks Portuguese to us.

I sometimes wish I had a Brazilian friend like him growing up. I would have felt less alone. There is this Brazilian kid who's my age in the enriched program at school (I'm in the regular one). His name is Rafael. He constantly spouts transphobic and homophobic BS, so I don't think it could ever work between us. Sometimes, when we pass each other in the school hall, we exchange looks, and it's like we *recognize* each other—we acknowledge how we are vulnerable in some similar ways. But there's also fire and shame and disgust. Sometimes I feel doomed to only experience an approximate sense of belonging.

We make it home after going through Maisonneuve Park, the one with the foxes and the rabbits, from the cycling freeway on Rachel Street—my dad always calls it that because during rush hour, the cycling path linking the upper Latin quarter to the East of Montréal becomes completely jam-packed; there are bicycles everywhere and people are extra impatient.

Virgil is already home to greet us. Just kidding, he's too busy playing *Minecraft* on our PC with his headphones on to even say "hi." While I start undressing as soon as I walk past the door, my dad manages to extract him from the game.

"How long have you been here? Did you even leave the house today?"

"Of course! I told you I'd be at Joáo's place. Then we came here to play with Borki and give him a walk. Joáo left an hour ago."

"Did you have fun?"

"Yeah. Did you?"

I jump into the discussion, entirely naked.

"It was so cool! We saw the hydroelectric dam and the locks in Beauharnois, and the maritime cycling path…."

"Aww! You went to see the locks without me?"

"You said you didn't want to come."

"Ha ha! That's right. I have no regrets, especially when I look at you right now."

I'm covered in sweat and dust, and my hair feels gross. I hurry to the shower after confirming with my dad that yes, Thai food sounds good, and yes, I'll have the bamboo special, as usual.

The food arrives and I'm too hungry to take the time to change into my pajamas, so I eat with just a towel wrapped around me. Having meals together is important in my family, but we don't really care for etiquette or good manners as long as we're all there.

While we eat, Virgil does all the talking because it's like that when he gets excited about something, and my dad and I are too exhausted.

"So, I told you that our Cub troop needs to raise money for the next camp, right? The winter camp. We're going to an adventure retreat in the mountains. It's going to be sweeeeet. Well, last Friday, the troop leader said, 'we need ideas for things we could do to raise money for the winter camp,' and I said 'how about we bake some cookies and pastries to sell them?' And the troop leader thought it a good idea, and João was all like 'yeaaaah.' But Léo said 'it's boring' and Noah—he's Léo's friend and he always sides with him even if it's actually Léo that's boring—he said, 'anyway, girl scouts already have a monopoly on cookies and pastries.' And the troop leader had to explain what a monopoly is, but he also said 'girl scouts don't have the monopoly on anything, anyone can sell cookies,' and then everyone started talking. They always do that, it gets a bit annoying sometimes, and I was there, raising my hand and waiting like at school because anyway, I couldn't speak loud enough, but it was too late. Bagheera, the troop leader, said, 'we're going to discuss it next week, think about it until then.'"

My brother joined the cubs a couple of months ago, because I was old enough to go to the youth meetings at the LGBT+ Center, but he wasn't, and that made him upset. He wanted some kind of weekly routine too. I'm not jealous, especially not when he starts telling us about the kind of stuff that happens at cub meetings. It's just irksome that I can't have anything for myself without him asking for some counterpart.

"So, anyway, João and I have been doing some thinking like we were supposed to, and this afternoon, his sister was out, and I said, 'Let's play *Drag Race*,' so we put on outfits—you should see that blue wig João has, it's hilarious. We took some pictures, they're on my phone. I'll show you later—and started working on acts, and that's when it dawned on me: We should have a drag show for the fundraiser! Like a talent show, but with drag queens and lip-sync battles and skits."

I admire my brother's enthusiasm but can't help being dubious.

"You're sure you can get a whole troop of cubs to get on board with doing a drag show? That sounds like a potential train wreck."

"Well, João and I are on board, and I know Gregory's parents let him watch RuPaul."

"Then good luck with that."

"Thanks! Also, I could be the emcee. Imagine—it would be Dolores von Tragic's time to shine!"

Dolores von Tragic is Virgil's drag persona. The character is the rich heir to a French canned tuna empire with a troubled past who decided to make a comeback after decades of being away from the public eye.

When we're done eating, Virgil begs me to help him take new pictures for Dolores von Tragic's Instagram account that I helped him set up. It got quite a lot of followers, especially since Lydia Dynamite, the drag queen who won *Canada's Got Talent*, tweeted about it. That really got Virgil into drag.

We choose a dress and some accessories for him and hang a satin curtain on his wall as a background for the pictures. People don't understand how he can pull out that diva attitude so easily. They are surprised I'm not the one into that kind of stuff. What can I say? He's a natural.

CHAPTER 3

"SO, WE WERE leaving our hotel and heading to the airport shuttle, a twenty-minute walk away. There was my coach, three other guys, and one of my teammates' dad, Mathieu, who volunteered to come, and I was only carrying my small suitcase. You know, that blue bag with four wheels that you can push instead of pulling it? Well, I was pushing it on the sidewalk, all chill, when all of a sudden, my mom messaged me. She wanted to know how the last competition went, so I started telling her about my teammate's broken toe. I think I already told you that part."

"Oh yeah. I still can't believe a rat led to that."

"Right?! It was so huge. Anyway, I get into it, you know how Leos like to boast, and my mom is all flabbergasted. We stop at a red light, and there's tons of people on the sidewalk. Typical New York afternoon. Since we have to wait a moment,

I use both of my hands to text my mom. I'm not much of a single-hand texting type of guy anyway, my thumb gets numb after a while. Then the light turns green, we start walking again, one block, two blocks, three blocks, all the way to the airport shuttle, and everyone starts loading their bags, and I'm just like, 'Hey…. My bag! I don't have my bag!' For a moment, I just look around, thinking some jackass was playing a trick on me, when I realize I've actually been walking this entire time without it! I left it at that red light!"

"Damn!"

"I start panicking, and you know me, I'm not one to do that."

"I'm not sure I've ever seen you even slightly stressed about anything."

"Exactly! But there was my sketchbook in that bag, and my meds, and my passport, and my favorite hoodie, everything. I tell my coach, 'Hey coach, I don't have my bag!' and he looks at me and he's like, 'What do you mean, you don't have your bag?' I tell him I think I forgot it a couple of blocks back, and he starts cursing, he's all like: 'What the heck, Liam!' You know, because it's New York, and it's full of people, and the airport shuttle is about to leave, and we have a flight to catch. Now we're both standing there. It's *super* tense. He asks the bus driver if he can wait a couple minutes, but he's on a tight schedule, and so are we, so the coach tells the other boys on the team to just go to the airport with Sasha's dad, Mathieu, and you could tell from that poor dude's face that it was every single one of his worst fears happening all at once.

Coach basically screams to him to take care of his bag and left it under the bus. It was kind of funny because we started sprinting, but Coach was still yelling to him, 'It's the burgundy bag with a perch on it! The burgundy bag with a perch on it!' And Mathieu was soooo confused, he had no clue burgundy was even a color and didn't understand what coach meant by 'perch,' but he meant the fish, of course."

"Of course."

"And then we run, I run like I've never ran, we jaywalk, we skip red lights, we don't take a single moment to catch our breath. I try to remember which corner I left my bag at, but it's hard, because I was texting and not paying attention at all, and have you ever been to New York?"

"Nope."

"It's just skyscrapers everywhere! Buildings, more buildings, pavement, a ton of Starbucks, some Panera Breads, more buildings. Every corner kind of looks the same, it's so intense. And the people! There's people everywhere."

"Like Toronto?"

"No, not really."

"Toronto is the only other city that I've been to. There were quite a few people. We went to São Paulo when I was a kid, but I don't remember anything."

"Oh. Anyway, we were just running all the way from where we came, trying to avoid the people, and I couldn't remember where I left my bag, and I started getting desperate about ever seeing it again. But as we were approaching the hotel, we bumped into a blockade, a perimeter of police officers, police cars with their sirens on, a special forces truck, and a yellow 'danger' tape, like in the movies. It looked really serious! We tried to go through, but someone screamed at us: 'You can't pass, there's a suspicious bag!' And I looked on the other side of the 'danger' tape, and guess what I saw?"

"Your bag?"

"Yes! They thought it was some sort of bomb! Someone wearing what looked a bit like a diver or an astronaut suit was getting out of the special forces truck with a bunch of complicated-looking equipment, ready to blow up my bag!"

"No way!"

"Yes way! I run to a police officer and I say, 'That's my bag!' He turns toward me, he looks so tired that he's not even upset, and he repeats what I said: 'That's your bag, really?' And I'm just so relieved it's still there, and I'm so happy it wasn't stolen or blown up already that I start laughing and crying tears of joy, and I want to hug the police officer, but he gets very defensive and shouts, 'Step back!'"

"I heard the police there can be a lot more rude than here."

"Yeah, especially with people of color. Anyway, that's when I took the selfie."

We hear from behind us, "What selfie?"

We turn around and Stephie takes off her school bag, making her way between Liam and me to the locker we share. Liam, who knows about our smooching session of Saturday, says hello to her and looks at me with a complicit smile.

"I was just telling Ciel about how the NYPD almost blew up my bag because they thought it was a bomb."

"Holy shit. How come that kind of stuff always happens to you?"

"I must be lucky! Anyway, we grabbed my bag and hopped in a cab to the airport. We arrived like two minutes before they closed check-in."

"That's hardcore."

I look at Stephie. She has something sadder than usual in her expression, something she probably tried to conceal with makeup and a fancy hairdo. She even has on a bit of eyeliner and mascara. It's rare that she wears makeup to school, but I guess this morning, she made an exception. She'll probably bump into Frank at some point during the day, and she'll want to look as if she has already moved on.

I fake an outraged voice when I notice her lips. "Hey, you're wearing our special gloss! We're supposed to tell each other when one of us wears it so we can match, remember?"

She opens her bag and takes the expensive lip gloss we both own out of her makeup pouch.

"I got your back. Sorry, I got up late and was in too much of a hurry to text you."

"I was just kidding. But thanks!"

I open our locker where I find the broken mirror that used to hang on the door before it fell off when Stephie slammed the door a bit too hard. While I apply the gloss, Liam says, "I guess I'll leave you to your business. I'll see you both in French!"

I turn to say bye, and I can see in his eyes that he imagines Stephie and I are going to get all touchy-feely once he leaves.

Stephie is busy emptying the content of her school bag into our locker and preparing her notebooks and pencil case for her first class. I have no clue how to handle this limbo. Are we supposed to kiss? She used to kiss Frank every morning, but it's not like she and I are actually dating, or even open about our relationship. Yesterday, after Virgil and I were done updating Dolores von Tragic's Instagram with new photos, Stephie and I spent hours messaging each other, but we didn't say a word about what happened on Saturday night. I didn't want to bring it up, since she's going through so much, but I'd really like to know *what* we are.

I ask her, "Did you manage to finish the book report?"

"Well, duh! What do you think kept me up last night?"

"I don't know, you seemed to have a lot on your mind."

"You mean after Frank left me that silly voicemail message? I did wonder if I should call him back, but it wasn't... you know. I wasn't anxious about it, just annoyed."

"I see."

"Trust me. I'm over it."

"Well, I'm not. I'm still so upset at him. And guess who's going to be in my science and technology class this morning?"

"Oh geez. Frank and Viktor."

"Yup. It's making me throw up in my mouth a little."

"I recommend ignoring them."

"It's going to be hard. I'm sitting right behind them, and I always overhear their little immature jokes."

"Ugh. I can't believe I've endured so much of that awful banter. Can't you switch places?"

"Not exactly. We don't have assigned seats, but everyone always sits at the same place since the beginning of the school year...."

Stephie's eyes shift to something behind me, and I turn my head. Raquel, Viktor's girlfriend who sent nudes to him, is coming in our direction with two of her friends. They walk with dignity, even though some people in the school hall, including Stephie and me, stop talking to watch. I wonder how many people know about the pictures.

The procession passes us by, and I try my best to look at Raquel in a way that shows her I'm on her side, even though I would never in any other circumstance be her friend, considering some of the nasty, transphobic things she has said in the past about Stephie and me. Also, she might not even realize that we know what happened.

The bell rings and people start moving toward their classrooms. I wish this whole story could die swiftly. I hope it fades away on the wind.

Stephie says good-bye but we both stay still. Then she leans toward me, and my heart starts to pound.

She hugs me.

"Thanks for being there for me."

"No worries, you'd do the same. By the way, can I read your book report? Just so that I can compare it to mine."

"I thought you haven't started it yet."

"I have the basic plan. I want to compare the structure."

"Since when do you make plans?"

★ ★ ★

The squishiness of Stephie's skin fuses in my mind with the mint and cucumber scent of the lotion she puts on before her makeup, and as I walk to my science and technology class, my senses can't decide if she smelled soft or if she felt fresh.

Frank and Viktor are already there, at their usual spot near the wall on the far left of the classroom. I do my best to avoid looking at them and go toward one of the tables in the back of the classroom, one row before the last one. I don't remember anyone sitting there, so I guess I will be fine.

I like our science and technology teacher, Nathaniel Brazeau. He's the youngest and hairiest teacher I have, and he always makes the best jokes. Apparently, he's in a band. Everyone at school is talking about it. Stephie also has a crush on him, and she's not even in his class. She told me she googled him and found his band, it's like punk rock. Some days, he says his throat hurts so much from the singing and screaming that he can't really teach, so we watch movies or do silent team-work instead (his throat injuries often come with headaches). Needless to say, he's very popular.

I'm all alone in the back of the classroom until a few seconds before the second bell, when a group of students walks through the door and surrounds me. One of them, the one with the coolest haircut, says to me, visibly annoyed, "That's my table."

There are four of them, and they seem to stay close to each other like a pack of stray dogs. I've noticed their faces before, but I'm not sure I know all of their names. I think the one with the cool haircut's name is Ivan or Dylan or something. I start putting my books back in a pile and my pens and markers back in my pencil case.

"I'm really sorry! I thought the seat was free."

"You better be sorry, faggot! Now we're late because of you."

I've heard that insult enough times to be immune to it. While I get up, I simply roll my eyes as some classmates turn around to see what the fuss is about. The worst part of it is that it forced me to make eye contact with Frank, who must definitely have noticed the trouble I'm putting myself through just so that I don't have to sit near him.

One of the other guys, who is so edgy that he wears a cap inside, delivers another blow as I'm trying to find another table. "Hurry up, sissy!"

"Shut up, Gabe!"

No need to look to see who it came from: it was clearly Frank's voice. I didn't ask him to do anything. He's who I was trying to avoid. Now it's just awkward.

There's a free seat near the door, at the front of the classroom, where the cheerleading squad sits. Well, not the entire cheerleading squad, obviously, but the three ninth-grade members. I would have preferred to have an entire table to myself, but whatever, the class is about to start. I go to Cynthia, who sits by herself while Jayden and Carolina share the table in front, and I ask her in a low voice, "Mind if I sit here?"

She smiles and removes her bag and her flowery jacket from the seat next to her, as an invitation for me to sit down. I whisper a meaningful "thank you" and let our teacher begin.

The cheerleading squad is obviously too cool for me. All the most popular girls are in it. They all have great style. I have great style too, and I think they acknowledge and respect it, but I'm probably too quirky to ever fit in. Anyway, I already have enough nerds to hang out with. I'm not envious.

I like Jayden. He's not really my friend and we probably don't have much in common, but it's nice to have someone else who's perceived as an effeminate boy around. I feel somewhat safer when he's there. Also, he has a way with people that I don't. He's charismatic.

Once the class has started and Mr. Brazeau is well settled into the subject (he's talking about some mechanical concepts), I subtly look over my shoulder to peek at the guys who rudely forced me to find another table. I see Cool Haircut dude on his phone. There's so much free space, every one of them has a table to himself. It's not fair. My eyes meet with Edgy Dude Wearing a Cap Indoors (Frank called him Gabe? Gabriel, probably). It's like he's guarding the area. From afar, he glares at me and raises his chin in an intimidating way. I know what that means: *What do you want?* I'm tempted to do it back at him, but I just sigh and turn my head.

CHAPTER 4

AT LUNCH, I sit with Stephie and her friends, as usual. I mean, they're also my friends, I guess, but I'm not sure it would be that simple if it wasn't for Stephie. The thing is, unlike her I don't think I can handle having more than two or three actual friends, and certainly not all at the same time. She's always surrounded by tons of people. I have no idea how she pulls that off. It would stress me. I basically only talk to Liam and her, and that's enough to exhaust me, socially speaking. Group discussions drain me, and I always end up listening without saying a word the whole time. I don't think it's anxiety, though. It's not that I'm scared to speak up or fear being judged. I simply crave intimacy. When I'm incapable of properly caring for everyone in the group, I feel powerless.

Sometimes I have lunch at Liam's house. He lives a couple of blocks away from the school, near the subway station. It's a change from the noise of the cafeteria and it allows us to have actual, full-length discussions (I can't stand small talk, it stresses me out), but the round trip between the school and Liam's house takes a big chunk of the lunch break, and we always end up having to eat super-fast. The main reason why he goes home every day is so he can use the bathroom in his house. He says the ones at school are the yuckiest things ever. Can't say I disagree. But yeah, I'd rather have lunch with Stephie and her friends than rush in and out of Liam's place every day.

I sit next to Stephie, like I always do, and I'm just appreciating the discussion without participating (they're all chatting about that TV dance show that I don't watch). Stephie's leg is touching mine, and I wonder if she's doing it on purpose, so I start gently kicking her foot. She plays along and kicks back. I kick again, and so does she, and that's actually really nice. I can feel the heat from her thigh, and it makes me forget about the noise and the yelling and the gravy smell mixed with the vanilla scent from the chocolate cookies. Samira, Stephie's friend that I know the best because she happens to be the school's Gender and Sexuality Alliance president, says, "Oh, did you hear the news? Apparently, Raquel broke up with Viktor. Her friend Elsa told me this morning."

"Fresh juicy drama!"

"It's a miracle those two lasted more than a week, in my opinion."

"I wouldn't last for more than a day with Viktor. He's a jerk. Sorry, Stephie, I know he's your boyfriend's best friend...."

I gasp and look at Stephie with big eyes.

"He's not my boyfriend anymore. We broke up Saturday."

Everyone stops chewing for a moment, and it's like the entire school becomes silent. Samira squeaks, "I'm so sorry, Stephie! I didn't know. Are you alright?"

Stephie shrugs and looks away. She doesn't seem to want to talk about it, but everyone at the table wants details. She says, "It's actually related to Raquel and Viktor. Raquel sent pictures…you know, pictures where you can *see* things."

"Nudes!"

"I can't believe she did that!"

"Don't blame her. Viktor probably pressured her to do it."

"Yeah. I bet that's why they broke up."

Stephie continues. "And he probably showed them to Frank because Frank had the guts to ask me for some too."

"Damn!"

"Report his ass to the police."

"That's nonsense. Frank won't be thrown in jail just for *asking* for nudes."

"Police! This guy is a turd!"

"That's not funny."

Stephie says, "Well, he didn't just *ask*. Let's say he *insisted*."

"Sorry, Stephie. It must be hard. You've been together for like, what? Thirty years?"

"One year and a half. Twenty months, actually."

"An eternity!"

"Yeah…."

Stephie goes quiet. You can feel the heaviness over the table, like a dark cloud bringing not much good. Samira struggles. "Let's…let's change the subject, shall we?"

"My mom got a new game for the Switch."

"Your mom is a geek. She has all the games."

While the others start talking about Leah's mom and how cool she is, I squeeze Stephie's hand. She seems to be battling tears. I whisper to her, "Do you want to take a walk? Go to the bathroom?"

She nods and excuses herself from the table. Leah says she'll keep an eye on her stuff. I take Stephie's hand and lead her out.

Once we're at the washroom, she washes her hands with cold water and takes deep breaths. I don't ask if she's okay. She says, "Putting on mascara was the worst idea ever. I'll end up looking like a racoon before the end of the day."

"Hey, don't say bad stuff about racoons! They're precious."

"Sorry. Do you think we should have a discussion?"

"Always! We're having one right now. What do you want to tell me?"

"Silly. I meant Frank and me."

"I don't know. Maybe you should take some time for yourself."

"Yeah, I would probably burst into tears if I was in front of him."

"I know you would. And he legit wouldn't understand a single word you'd say anyway."

"Ha ha ha! You're right."

She sniffles. She's way less over it than I thought. A girl comes out of a stall and watches us suspiciously. We don't say a word until she walks out. I ask, "Wanna come do homework at my place after school?"

"Are you saying that so you can copy my book report?"

"Hmmmm…. Maybe?"

"Give me one good reason why I should let you do that."

"Well, first, because I didn't read the book."

"Geez, Ciel! Really?"

"Yes. Second, I don't have time to do it because I'm busy picking up the shattered pieces of your broken heart."

"Legit. Alright. I'll come."

We agree to meet at our locker when school is over. She wipes her hands and hugs me very tightly. Another girl comes in and gives us an even weirder look, but we don't care.

The prospect of hanging out really helps me get through the afternoon (I have math and field hockey practice, it's long and painful). Stephie is already at our locker when I arrive from phys ed—not a surprise, considering the time it takes me to change since I always wait until there's no one left in the changing rooms before going inside—a survival tactic that I developed in elementary school. The bell had already rung.

We put our jackets on our backs, our school bags on our shoulders, our umbrellas in our hands, and we head out. It would probably be faster to take the city bus, but they're always so crowded at this time that even Stephie feels overwhelmed. I walk or cycle home most of the time.

We stroll slowly on the sidewalk, which is a tiny bit too small for two people to walk side by side with umbrellas. We purposefully make them bounce against each other, as a game. She tells me, "I like walking in the rain."

"I'm mostly glad it's not pouring like this morning."

"Yeah, it's perfect."

"Just like you."

"Aww!"

I wink at her, and she replies with the sweetest smile. As we walk by a dépanneur, she has an epiphany. Grabbing my arm, she whispers, as if we were about to rob the corner store at gunpoint, "Let's buy candy before going to your place. It's called 'self-care.' I made good money babysitting last week."

I laugh. When we're inside, she says to pick some for myself too and she'll pay, but I only pick the ones I know we both like. We also grab two sodas and pay at the counter. She looks me dead in the eye and says, "We can't let your brother see these. He won't stop annoying us until we share."

"You know him very well! Put them in my bag."

As soon as we open the door to my apartment, Borki jumps on Stephie and licks her. They are huge fans of each other. Stephie's dad has always been allergic, and her mom feels she's out of the city too often to take care of a pet, so she's never had any. Since her parents are divorced, she can't really have one by herself.

Virgil follows our dog and gets as excited as Borki when he sees Stephie. She has a way with kids, too: she's always babysitting and wants to become an elementary school teacher.

There's something about her that is so soft and soothing. I can understand why children like her so much. I don't know if it's feigned, but when Virgil talks to her, it's like what he says is the most amazing and interesting thing in the world. Stephie's eyes become all sparkly. Even though he's not a baby anymore, you can tell Virgil is thrilled to feel like he's the most miraculous wonder in the world again.

"Stephie, guess what! With the cub scouts, we might do a drag show to raise funds for our winter camp."

"That's so awesome! Will you be Dolores von Tragic?"

"Of course!!"

Stephie's subscribed to his profile. I say, "Calm down, Virgil, you didn't even tell the idea to your troop yet, and it hasn't been approved."

"I'm going to do it on Friday. And I'm sure it will pass because it's the best idea ever."

"What will you tell them?"

"Well, that our fundraiser could be like a talent show, but funnier."

"Maybe you should play on the shock factor."

"What does that mean?"

"If you tell your troop that more people would be interested in the fundraiser because of how revolutionary it would be, it might convince the ones that don't like the idea."

"I don't understand."

"Think of the scandal: cub scouts putting on a drag show! I'm sure newspapers would talk about that."

"Why would it be a scandal? I don't get it."

"Because boy scouts are supposed to be all manly. Manly! Arrr! But then you go there and put on a drag show, which has been used as an art form for centuries to subvert masculinity and traditional gender roles. It's the bomb!"

"Yeah! A bomb!! Thank you for the advice. I'll tell them."

Virgil starts jumping around and goes back to the computer, where he was watching some dance tutorial. Stephie smiles at me. I know she thinks Virgil is the most adorable cutie-patootie in the world, but in reality, he's a demonic, evil, smelly brat.

"I'm sure he didn't understand a word you said."

"Meh. Whatever. I hope this drag show happens. It would be hilarious."

We go to my room and unpack our treasure on the bed. I gulp down my cream soda while Stephie takes her new pink portfolio out of her bag. She keeps all her homework and projects in it. She's had the habit of doing that for as long as I've known her. Stephie, monarch of order and organization. During most of her elementary years, you could see her walking around school with her old portfolio, which had dolphins jumping out of the water in the sunset on it. The new one isn't as tacky, but it's still a little bit childish, and I love her for it.

She opens it and finds her book report, a three-page document that she throws at me in defiance.

"Make good use of it."

"I won't disappoint you!"

"I have some math exercises to do. Just ask if there's something you don't understand."

I read in silence. After a few moments, I shout, "What?! The character's first husband was *murdered*? Spoilers much!"

"Don't ask to read my book report if you don't want to be spoiled!"

"That's okay, I won't read the book. Did they make a movie out of it?"

"I'm not sure. Maybe?"

I manage to get through Stephie's report, which is very good, informative, well-structured, and full of complicated words. From what I gathered, the book is about a woman who, on the deathbed of her second husband, recollects memories from when she and her secret lover murdered her first husband, and it's only at the end that we can get the full picture and the seemingly unrelated elements start making sense. I'm surprised our French teacher, Ms. Campeau, is making us read such a gory book.

I go back and forth between the three pages of Stephie's book report, trying to absorb as much information as I can to make it seem like I read the book without sounding like Stephie. It shouldn't be too hard, I'm a pro at this. I ask her, "Do you know when's the last day to hand in our book report?"

"I think it's in two weeks."

"Perfect. Then you should give yours to the teacher tomorrow, and I'll give mine on the last day. She'll have time to forget about yours by the time she gets to mine."

"Oh! I'm the teacher's pet. There's no way she can forget any word that originated from my fantastic mind."

"I like how you totally own it."

"It's just facts. Cold, hard facts."

"Such a model student!"

"Don't be blinded by my performance. I'm far from being a model student. The truth is that I just show up and like to read. I never study, and I'm having an awful time with this math homework right now."

"Yeah, yeah, sure. You just don't like when I point out how great you are."

"I'm bad with compliments, okay?"

She throws a pillow at me. I laugh. "Be careful! You'll crush your book report!"

"Well, I don't care."

"Such a badass!"

"Am I rebel enough to lose that model student title, now?"

"Not a chance."

She grumbles and goes back to her homework. Talking about model and rebel students reminded me of the events from this morning, in biology. I stay quiet a moment, remembering how mean that boy with the cool haircut was, that stare from Gabriel. These guys probably think they're badasses and rebels too.

"You know, I'd rather you were a huge nerd than someone who'd be called a rebel by people at school."

"That's inaccurate. I'm not huge, I'm chubby."

"Sorry, chubby nerd."

"That's better. Why do you say that?"

"These guys in my class today, they thought they were being tough, but they were mostly just throwing a tantrum because I sat in one of their seats. I was trying to move as far as I could from Frank and Viktor."

"What happened?"

"One of them got angry at me for sitting there. He called me a faggot."

"So edgy. So original."

"Then that other one, who was just following the first guy, he just had to call me a sissy even though I said I was sorry and had already picked up my things."

"Humans are awful."

"Hey, hashtag not-all-humans. We have some human friends, remember?"

"Yeah, human allies to our divine selves."

"Anyway. He kept…staring at me during class. I really pissed him off even though I didn't do anything. I was so uncomfortable."

"Maybe it was his first time being knowingly so close to a gay and that was enough for him to feel threatened in his masculinity?"

"I don't know. But he was wearing his hockey hat inside."

"That's something I could do. Wearing a hat inside. That's easy."

"You'd finally be a True Rebel™!"

"Hey, I think I'm done with my math homework."

"Noice. What do you want to do?"

"Eat candy!"

She crawls on the bed to reach the licorice bag I've been eating from since we arrived.

"Empty?!"

"I couldn't resist! I'm sorry."

"That's not fair. How can you always eat so much junk and stay so thin?"

"I don't know. I cycle a lot?"

She opens a bag of candy worms and sighs. "I should exercise more. I feel so fat."

"Well, you're chubby. And cute. And there's nothing wrong with being fat."

"I should probably care more about that stuff, now that I'm not with Frank anymore."

"Why? I already think you're the prettiest girl in our grade."

"Aww! Stop it."

"Make me."

I put my hand on hers. She looks at me delightfully. The blood rushing to my face probably makes me a lot redder. And then we stop moving for a moment, just feeling each other breathing. I bite my lip and manage to ask, "Do you want to cuddle?"

Stephie's smile changes. She leans toward me and says, "I do. But this time, no kissing, alright?"

That answer surprises me since I wasn't exactly thinking about kissing. But okay, whatever.

"Just cuddling is great. That's what I said anyway."

"I know. Just making sure."

We both lie down on top of my blanket and start hugging. I've been thinking about this since I left her arms, a couple of days ago. Except that this time, it's like there's no urgency, no rush. I say, "This is nice."

"Yeah."

We stay like that for a couple of minutes, squeezing each other's body and exchanging heat. She whispers, "I need to tell you…I think it was a mistake, what we did on Saturday. We shouldn't kiss. We're best friends."

I turn cold.

"Best friends can kiss, it's not illegal."

"I'm not saying it is, but that we shouldn't…. I just broke up with Frank. I'm not sure what I want right now. It's confusing."

"But it was nice, wasn't it?"

"It was. And I would definitely want to kiss you again."

"Ten out of ten, would kiss again."

"I'm serious. I'm not ready for anything. And I especially don't want to hurt you. Oh…look at you. I did hurt you. I'm sorry. I'm so sorry."

"It's fine. I'm fine."

She hugs me tighter. It helps with keeping the tears inside. I sigh and say, "We can still cuddle, can't we?"

"We can."

"I have bad news, though."

"What is it?"

I reach behind me and pull something from under my leg.

"I think you'll have to reprint your book report."

CHAPTER 5

"YOU'RE SUCH a Taurus. Personally, I think it's a weird idea to fall in love when the glaciers are melting and the planet is becoming more hostile to humans every day."

Liam is like that. You try to say something cute about love and butterflies and he drops the most apocalyptic scenario he can think of.

"Why? It would make it more bearable."

"It's a distraction. Next thing you know, you'll want to start a family and you'll burden kids with saving a planet that the richest one per cent scrapped, all in the name of love. It's selfish."

"Your heart is made of stone, that's why."

"No shit! I'm a Leo. What do you think?"

It always surprises me how Liam can be so down-to-earth on one hand, and so esoteric on the other. He knows everything about astrology and zodiac signs. When he's having a bad day, it's always the fault of some constellation or because Mercury is in retrograde or something like that. I don't really understand his obsession.

As we walk to French class, he continues. "Take yourself, a Taurus. Tauruses need romance. Not because of attraction or compulsion, just romance for the sake of it. You gotta work on that. You're burning with the *desire to desire*. You're doing yourself a disservice by letting it take over. It consumes you."

"It's not like having a crush on my best friend was making me unable to function. I got up and made myself breakfast this morning! An omelet, of all things."

"Fancy. But how did you sleep?"

"…Not so well, I guess."

"I knew it! You're too intense."

"And I shouldn't tell you anything."

"We all have our weak spots. You like being in love, I like watching the drama. Win-win."

"I don't 'like being in love.' Quite the opposite, actually."

In the classroom, Liam and I sit at our desks near the door. I smile at Ms. Campeau, our teacher, and wave at Stephie, sitting with some girls near the windows. When she sees me, she pulls out her hot pink portfolio from her bag, gets up, and walks to the teacher's desk to hand in what is probably her book report, which she must have reprinted. Then she winks at me and goes back to her seat. She's so cute, it hurts.

Liam reads the horoscope in the free daily *Metro* news-paper in silence, while I think about what he said about desire to desire. Am I really like that? I don't fall in love easily, that's the thing. Stephie, on the contrary, has a new crush every other day. She eyes anyone who is a bit stronger or taller than she is. Sometimes, she doesn't even know their name. I'm glad it's not like that between us. I can't be just a fad. I know her inside out.

Thinking of it, I have been very close to every single one of my love interests before developing a crush on them. Is that a thing? We never hear about that anywhere. Love at first sight doesn't ring any bells to me. I don't think I've ever experienced it. I have to trust someone deeply before I even consider *liking* them.

There was Anthony, in second and third grade. We kept saying we would marry each other (no wonder my parents thought I was gay). We were always holding hands and it seemed so natural. It makes me a bit sad that we haven't spoken to each other in years. He got angry at me for some silly reason, and when my mom died, I think he felt really bad for me but didn't want to bring it up, and it got very awkward. We went our separate ways.

Of course, there was my first real boyfriend, Eiríkur. We loved hanging out way before we started dating. I'm the one who asked him out, because I couldn't get enough of him. I wanted more reasons for us to spend time together. What I liked the most about our relationship was how easy and comfortable it was. I guess I like routines. But he had to move back to Iceland....

Then it was Liam. I'm so glad it didn't make things weird between us. I still dream about him, sometimes. He's always been so nice to me, ever since we started talking after I recognized him from the newspaper—he made the headlines because some people thought it was unfair that a trans person could participate in swimming competitions while using hormone treatment. I had liked how chill and laid back he always was before I developed any feelings for him. Right now, for example, I wish I could just hold his hand in the classroom like I would have done with Anthony, in second grade.

But how do I know if it was actually love, in any of these cases? What if the thing I thought was love was just an attempt to seal some imaginary friendship pact? I have never had many friends, yet I always seem to find a way to fall in love with every single one of them.

Liam pulls me out of my daydream by sliding the folded newspaper over to my side of the table. He circled the horoscope for Taurus. It says, "Don't let challenging times get to you. Remain open to every opportunity." I take a pen out of my bag and add at the bottom, "Welcome to Vague Town!"

★ ★ ★

At lunch, on my way to the cafeteria, I bump into the cheerleading squad. Cynthia and Carolina both look happy to see me. They're always so extra. Jayden waves shyly and I wave back. Carolina, with her smile that goes all the way from one ear to the other, asks, "Alex! How was your weekend?"

"Oh, it was great. My dad and I went cycling on the South Shore, we saw the dam, it was really s—"

"That's awesome!"

"Yeah. How about y—?"

"Catch up later! You should sit with us sometimes."

They disappear in the crowd. As much as I like them, they confuse me so much. Why would they ask me how my weekend was if they weren't interested in my answer? People do that. I don't get it. It was kind of rude, but at the same time, they invited me to join them. What am I supposed to think? Maybe they were just in a hurry. The line for the microwaves can get pretty long....

Yeah. Probably the microwaves.

I find our usual table. When Stephie sees me, she smiles and makes some space next to her.

There's something off with Stephie that I can't really pinpoint. She doesn't seem angry or anything, but it's like she's avoiding interacting too much with me. I know, it's ironic coming from someone who usually spends the entire lunch break not saying a word, only laughing at the right moments. But I can't help worrying about her, and the tension makes me nervous.

She seemed perfectly fine with cuddling the other night. And we didn't kiss, just like she wanted. We haven't really talked since then, except at the locker after French class, when she told me how unsurprised the teacher was that she was the first to hand in her book report. Maybe that's what she's upset about? Sometimes she has complicated feelings like that. Is she even upset? I can't read her right now.

As Leah offers us a poignant speech about why some generic, white, short-haired guy shouldn't get to the finals of that reality show she watches (I agree with her, he sounds like a jerk), my horoscope from this morning, of all things, pops up into my head. How did it go again? "Challenging times, grab opportunities?" What if it was about that, precisely? Not about mediocre guys, but about my crush on Stephie, which seems like it will only make things awkward between us, and the invitation from the cheerleading squad? Maybe I should sit with them tomorrow. It would be refreshing.

The bell rings, and everyone leaves the cafeteria. Stephie finally says something to me. "You're going to math, right? My social science class is also on the second floor, let's go together."

I'm glad she asks. I reply, "I have a notebook to pick up, it's in the locker."

"I can come, I'll drop my lunchbox at the same time."

I accept, and we walk in silence. I hope I don't look too nervous. Going down the stairs, I am suddenly pushed toward the ramp, and my body spasms while I'm trying to understand what's happening. Stephie yells, and I look up and see that boy with the cool hair from my science and technology class, followed by that Gabriel person, still wearing his hat indoors. Is he afraid that neon lights might give him a sunburn? Stephie shouts at them, "You could just say you're sorry!"

"He was in the way."

"They weren't!"

A couple of students stop when they hear Stephie, expecting some kind of fight. I look at Stephie and just nod my head lightly, with my eyes saying, *It's not worth it.* She squeezes my hand, and we make our way to the lockers. She's biting her lip so hard that all the upper part of her chin is turning red. Stephie can be scary when she enters Mama Bear mode.

We arrive at our locker, and I try to find my math notebook quickly. Stephie looks at the end of the hall, her arms crossed. I say, "It was the same guys from yesterday, in my class. The ones who made me change desks."

"What's their problem anyway? What's their deal?"

I throw my hair behind my shoulders. "They can't handle my fabulousness."

"They missed the sparkle train."

"Haters gonna hate."

"Etcetera, etcetera."

"Got my notebook. Let's go."

We go back upstairs without saying anything. I wish she would take my hand like she had a couple of minutes ago, but she's the one who still looks upset, not me. When we finally arrive at my classroom, she says, "You're alright?"

"Yeah."

"You're sure?"

"Yeah. You?"

"I'm alright. See you later."

We blow each other kisses because we're that cool.

★ ★ ★

When I arrive home after school, I find Virgil practicing some dance moves in his cub outfit, except he's wearing a tutu (that used to belong to me) instead of pants. Now, I don't know much about cubs or dancing, but I'm pretty sure this wouldn't be approved as a uniform. His dance is simultaneously terrible and awesome. His moves are exaggerated, which I guess is a prerequisite for drag.

"Can you turn the volume down?"

"Nope! But I'll go take Borki on a walk shortly, so be patient, dearest sibling."

Because the volume is so loud, Virgil has to scream that sentence to me. Borki rushes into the living room barking.

"No! Not now. Later. La-ter!"

But Borki starts jumping on him, and there's no way he'll be able to practice anything anymore, so he stops the video, laughs, and throws himself on the carpet to roll with our dog. I think for a moment then proclaim, "Hey, it's nice out. I'll go with you."

"Did you hear that, Borki? Did you hear that? Ciel's coming with us!"

I drop my bag near the couch and watch as my brother gets up and struggles to put on his shoes through the puffy frills of the tutu.

"You're gonna wear that to the park?"

"What do you think? I won't go in underwear!"

"That wasn't what I was suggesting. You usually butch it up a little whenever you go outside."

"Dolores von Tragic does what she pleases!"

"Of course."

We put Borki's leash on and grab some toys before heading out. Borki is so excited that he skips many steps on the stairs.

"He really needed to go! Why were you keeping him waiting?"

"He was sleeping. Plus, I wanted to rehearse in case they ask me to perform on Friday."

"At your cub meeting?"

"Yeah. What if I tell them about my idea, and they want a sample of what it could look like? I'll come prepared."

"I don't think…. Okay, sure, that's a possibility."

When we're outside, Virgil jumps and twirls around. He's probably adorable, I don't know. That's what people always say. It makes me quite bitter because his whole deal is pretty much just imitating me, but when I was his age, I was just a weirdo who made people uncomfortable. I guess he has more charisma than me, like Jayden. He makes friends way more easily than I do, that's for sure. Maybe that will save him from bullying. Who knows? I hope so.

The Maisonneuve Park, right by our apartment, is perfect to play with Borki: many trees and fields, and not a lot of other dogs or people, especially at this time of the year. Tourists like it in the summer because it's so close to Montréal's Olympic Tower, but most of them would freeze to death right now, so they're nowhere to be seen. It's a shame, because the entire park turns various shades of red, violet, and orange this time of year. Mixed with the emeraldish-blue of the spruces, it's breathtaking.

I throw a ball as far as I can and yell, "Go fetch!"

Borki starts running at full speed and almost trips over his own paws. Virgil laughs as our dog recovers the ball and brings it back to him. He throws it again and says, without looking at me, "You should come more often. It's fun."

I haven't come to the park with them in several weeks. Probably since I started ninth grade, actually.

"I know. I've been busy with all the drama."

"What drama?"

I think about the photos and Stephie's breakup. I sigh.

"You wouldn't understand."

He turns his head toward me. "Stop saying that. I'm not a baby."

"Alright, then. I think you already understand. You understand so well that it would be a waste of time and energy to explain it to you. We're like…connected."

"You're right. Thank you for trusting me."

He gets closer and gives me a surprise hug. Then he says, "I'm glad we talked."

"Me too."

"You can always tell me anything."

"Aww! Well then, I think you smell particularly bad today."

"HEY!"

He tries to tackle me, but I catch him and start tickling him until he's on the ground. That's when Borki comes back, fast as lightning, to save his master and jump in the melee.

"You said anything!"

"You know what I meant."

When we're too exhausted from laughing, we both stay on the grass for a moment to catch our breath. That's when two little girls approach us. We sit up as one of them asks, pointing at Borki, "Is that your dog?"

"Yup."

"Is it a boy or a girl?"

"We don't know, Borki doesn't talk yet."

"Oh."

They stare at us for a moment.

"Are you boys or girls?"

Virgil and I exchange a quick look, and say in perfect harmony, with the deepest and most guttural voices we can, "We're your worst nightmare."

The two girls scream and run away to the other end of the park, while we laugh our asses off again.

★ ★ ★

In the evening, I get a call from Liam. It's highly unusual. We both hate unannounced phone calls and always text the other one first before calling if we really need it.

"Hey."

"Hey, Ciel. What's up?"

Something in his voice makes me believe he doesn't really care about what is actually up.

"Well, uh, not much, just finished dinner. What about you?"

"I don't know. Have you seen the email?"

"What email?"

"Go look in your inbox. There should be an email from someone named Charles Tremblay. DO NOT OPEN IT."

"Alright, give me a second...."

I look at my phone, get to the main menu, and select the email app. Nothing new. I refresh, and there it is, one new email from Charles Tremblay, with "Important" as the subject. I put the phone back to my ear. "Yeah, it's there. What is it about?"

"Delete it right away."

"Is it a virus?"

"Worse."

He goes silent. I ask again, "What is it?"

"It's Raquel's nudes."

CHAPTER 6

THE NEXT MORNING, the name of the email's sender was on everybody's lips. "Charles Tremblay." Nobody knew who it was, not even Samira. When I talk to her at the lockers, Stephie is categorical. "It sounds fake. It must be an alias. I bet it's Viktor. He probably did it because Raquel broke up with him."

"Have you seen them?"

"Viktor and Raquel? I haven't. But someone in the group chat said she saw her in her morning class."

"That's courageous. Good for her. But I meant the pictures. Did you open the email?"

Stephie's face looks sorry.

"I did. And I saw. I couldn't stop crying, after."

She pauses and looks pensive.

"I feel so bad for Raquel."

"Same."

In second period, I have music class with Viktor. I spy on him from the back of the classroom, the assigned spot for the tuba player. (Our music teacher thinks it's really funny that I play the tuba because the marching band equivalent of the tuba is a sousaphone, and my last name is Sousa. Personally, I chose it because I'm one of the shortest in the class, and that instrument is huge. I like contrasts, and the effect is much funnier than "Alex Sousa on the sousaphone," or maybe it isn't, I'm not sure. I'm a bad judge of what's funny or not.)

During the entire class, people are chattering with Viktor. They drown him in questions. I hear him repeating that he didn't do it, that he is as shocked as everyone, and that he would never have let that happen. I don't know if I believe him or not. But that's not the most important thing: he shouldn't have shared those pictures with anyone in the first place. Raquel trusted him with them.

When it's finally time for lunch, I pass by the table where I usually sit with Stephie and the others. I tell them that I'll be eating with the cheerleading squad today, for a change. Stephie says, as a joke, "Oh! We totally understand, they're so much cooler than us."

If she wasn't my friend, the sarcasm might have gone way over my head, but she is, and we just start laughing.

"See you in French!"

I get to the table where Caroline, Cynthia, and Jayden are sitting with some older cheerleaders that I've never met. Suddenly, I remember I have social anxiety, and my entire body wants to do a U-turn, but it's too late, Cynthia sees me and waves. "Hey! Alex! Want to sit with us? There's a free seat here between Jayden and me."

She pushes Jayden and squeezes herself against the person on her other side. In fact, there is no free seat, it's more like a loophole. I look at the tiny space a moment. It's probably really uncomfortable. But it's too late to go back.

"Sure. Thanks!"

"No big deal. We were just talking about Raquel's pictures. Have you seen them?"

"I didn't."

"I did."

"Me too."

"Not me. Cynthia told me not to open it."

"You mean I saved your innocence. Some people in grade ten and eleven saw them."

"If I knew who sent those pictures, I would kick their butt so hard."

A boy with stubble, who I believe to be one of the older girls' boyfriends, jumps in. "What if she did it herself? It's crazy what people do for attention. I've heard of that happening before."

"Have you seen her? She's miserable. All the guys are making fun of her."

"You never know. And no one has heard of a Charles Tremblay."

Jayden, who hasn't said a word since I arrived, explodes. "She wasn't there in my math class earlier. She left between first and second period. She couldn't stand all the stares and the mocking. And you think she did it herself?"

"Yeah, seriously. Shut your mouth, Cliff."

"The kids are right."

"We're speculating, here. It's just one of the rumors."

"It's a shitty one."

The atmosphere is getting toxic. I want to change the subject but besides my three classmates, I don't know anyone here, and I want to give a good impression. So, I just wait. The group, which is taking up two whole cafeteria tables, or maybe even three, starts dividing itself into small factions, each talking about different things. Caroline turns toward me—we're sitting so close that her shoulder pushes mine in the process—and asks me, "You play any sports, Alex?"

"Sports? Not really. I like cycling."

"Ever thought about joining the cheerleading squad? Extra-curriculars give you great mentions in your report card. We could use more…muscles."

I get the feeling she was about to say "boys" but corrected herself in time. But to be honest, I would rather be called a boy than being told I'm muscular. It makes me feel gross. I laugh it off and explain, "I'm already part of Montréal's LGBT+ Youth Group. We do weekly meetings. That's already a lot for me."

"LGBT+ Youth Group? It sounds cool. You should go, Jay."

Jayden shrugs.

"Not really my thing. I don't like parades and making signs and shouting in the streets."

I laugh.

"That's not really a thing you'll see at the meetings. We mostly just eat food and chill. Sometimes there's a movie. It's a space to meet other queer and trans folks."

"That does sound nice. But I'm sure my parents wouldn't let me, anyway."

"Why not?"

"They don't know I'm gay. I'm not out."

My jaw drops. I keep forgetting it's a thing. I've never not been out. Being closeted isn't an option for me, my queerness emanates from every pore of my skin. I was under the impression that that was Jayden's case as well since his being gay is public knowledge at school. I guess I was wrong.

"May I ask why? Do you think they'd react badly?"

"Um, no. I don't want to talk about it. Not here. Not now."

"Oh. Sorry!"

Caroline and Cynthia proceed to ask me tons of random questions about the things I like and dislike. They mock me gently for being into the *Lafontaine* musical, saying it's a very nerdy thing to enjoy. I don't hold it against them.

"Hey, you should come see us cheer someday. Our first routine for the season is really getting on point," says Cynthia.

"Yeah, that would be great! No one ever comes to see us. It's always all about the sports teams," adds Caroline.

"When are you performing?"

"There's a basketball game next Monday. Then a soccer game next weekend."

"I'll think about it. Thanks for the invitation!"

Jayden didn't say a word after he mentioned that he didn't want to talk about the reasons he's not out to his parents. I thought he was upset with me, or annoyed at best. But maybe he isn't, because at the end of lunch he asks me if we can trade numbers. Caroline overhears him and tells Cynthia, "Yes! I knew we could do it."

They high-five. Jayden sighs very loudly. "Are you trying to set us up?"

Caroline giggles. "Maybe."

"Get out! Why would you do that?"

Cynthia replies, "Well duh, look at you two. You'd be amazing together. You could be the Winter Ball's couple! Jay, you'd be the king, and Alex could be, uh...."

"The co-sovereign."

"Yes, the co-sovereign, precisely. We even thought of a ship name for you two!"

"Do I want to hear it?"

"JAYDEX! Too late, now you know."

Jayden starts blushing, which is very obvious because of how light his skin is. It's like he pumps up the energy in his face before throwing it back. "I just thought it'd be nice to talk to someone going through some of the same stuff as me, okay? Also, Jaydex sounds like Pokédex. And Alex isn't really my type. No offense."

"None taken."

"But you said you thought they were cute the other day!"

"Well yeah, they are definitely cute. I mean, just look at them."

All the heads turn toward me, and it's my turn to blush. When they start commenting on my clothes and the things they like about them, I point to my smartphone and stutter, before disappearing. "Ha…ha…I'll…I'll text you, Jay… Jayden. I'll text you after school. See you later!"

★ ★ ★

I spend the rest of the day recovering. I'm not sure what to think about Caroline and Cynthia trying to match up Jayden and me (or should I say Jaydex?). It was sneaky and probably explains why they have been so nice to me lately, but I did end up with Jayden's number, so there's that.

I never imagined what it would be like to date him, which is unsettling because it's not the first time people have shipped us. It's probably because I don't know him so well. We don't have much in common except being both perceived as effeminate boys. We hang out with very different crowds. However, I wouldn't mind if something happened. He's nice and he thinks I'm cute.

After school, while I'm at home and waiting to leave for the LGBT+ Youth meeting, I decide to text him. I write and erase dozens of drafts, finally settling on,

Hey! I hope I didn't make things weird at lunch. You wanted to talk about stuff?

I get a reply thirty minutes later, as I'm on the way to the bus stop.

Sorry, I had cheer practice. Don't worry about it, seriously. It's Caroline and Cynthia who should be ashamed. Yeah, well, I didn't have anything precise in mind, I just thought it would be nice to have a chat in private.

So I can teach you all I know about how to gay?

Ha ha! Yes, please teach me, gay elder.

That sounds so wrong!

I know!!!

I arrive at the subway's green line, where I lose signal for my phone between a couple of stations. When I emerge at the iconic Beaudry station, in the heart of Montréal's Village, I sit down by the station's window and wait for Liam. He has swimming practice on Wednesdays, and we usually meet there before heading to the meeting. I must be the only teenager in this city with so much free time.

My phone eventually catches up with the signal, and I get a new message from Jayden.

I'm free tonight. Wanna do homework?

I can't. It's the LGBT+ Youth meeting.

Oh. Right. Tomorrow after school, then?

That could work.

Awesome! I'll text you my address. Talk to you later!

Bye!

I put my phone away and start reading a graphic novel Liam suggested to me. He's trying hard to get me into comics and mangas, but I have too much trouble focusing. I figure he might like to see me reading books he recommended, though.

Over the pages of the book, I catch sight of some kids who attend the meeting. They're easy to spot: most of them have bright, dyed hair. I like just being there and looking at the people coming and going from Beaudry station. It's where all the most colorful people of the city meet.

Montréal's modern-day Village is situated between the Latin Quarter and the Canadian Broadcasting tower, in the French-speaking part of town. A couple of years ago, one of the volunteers at the LGBT+ Center gave us a historical walking tour. It was one of the last things I did with my ex-boyfriend, Eiríkur, before he went back to Europe with his parents.

I remember there used to be two other known gayborhoods in the city: the Red Light district, around Sainte-Catherine and the Main, which had been there since at least 1920, and a LesboTown near the Mont-Royal station, up on the Plateau. They both moved to Beaudry in the Eighties, after the riots that followed the police raids on two gay clubs led to recognizing sexual orientation as a human right in Quebec's constitution. The rent in the area was a lot cheaper due to the damage done by the "Weekend Rouge" in 1974, when a series of fires spread at the same time that Montréal's firefighters were on strike. Entire blocks were burnt to the ground before they decided to put the strike on hold. Quite the story.

But now that the place is trendy, the rent is becoming so expensive that only the rich gays can afford to stay here. They're installing cameras everywhere, so young trans and queer people can be monitored by the police at any time, and of course people of color pay the highest price for it. That's one of the reasons why I'd rather not walk here alone, even when the place is swarming with tourists coming to see the multicolored balls hanging in the sky or the art installations to commemorate the AIDS epidemic.

Liam eventually arrives. His hair is still damp from the swimming pool. I wave at him and put the book back in my bag.

"Oh! That's *Drama*. How do you like it?"

"It's great. I like the characters."

"Yeah, I thought you would. It's Telgemeier at her finest. Much better than her first two books, in my opinion. It's underrated."

"Should I read them too?"

"Depends how you like that one."

We exit Beaudry station and walk a bit on Sainte-Catherine Street. Liam stops me. "Talking about comics, can we do a quick trip to the bookstore? I want to see if they have the new volume of *Lumberjanes*."

"Sure!"

Lumberjanes is the next thing Liam wants me to read. Apparently, it's a series with badass girls and gender non-conforming kids in a forest full of creatures.

Even though I don't read much, I like the atmosphere in L'Euguélionne, the small feminist and LGBTQIA+ bookshop in the Village. They have a zine section full of works from local artists and cool stickers and patches. I wish I had a job so I could buy them all. While Liam browses the comic section, I find a patch with the trans flag that says "Trans Liberation," and I decide that I need it. I show it to Liam. "What do you think?"

"It's perfect. Get it."

"Did you find the book you were looking for?"

"Nah, no luck."

Someone with green hair, behind the counter, overhears us and says, "We can order it for you, if it's not there."

Liam accepts and gives the title he wants to the person, who gets very enthusiastic about it.

"Awesome! I love these. You've got great taste!"

"Thank you."

They look it up online and take Liam's number to call him when it arrives, then I pay the two dollars and thirty cents for my patch, and we leave. I'm excited to sew it on my backpack. I already have two patches there: a Cookie Cat one from *Steven Universe* and the logo for Against Me, Laura Jane

Grace's band that I went to see with my dad a year ago when they were in Montréal. I always get nice comments when I'm walking with my bag.

We arrive at the LGBT+ Center and get to the room where the youth drop-in happens. I recognize many of the usual faces, and Liam and I say hello to some regulars we've come to know better over time.

Liam waves at Nathan, a fifteen-year-old gay guy from the South Shore of Montréal, who travels two hours by bus every week to attend these meetings. There's no such thing in his area.

"Hey, Nathan! Can we sit here?"

"Hey, Liam! Of course. How's life?"

Nathan didn't have to ask twice. Liam starts telling him everything about his experience with New York's police department. I listen vaguely and giggle at the right moments—I'm starting to know that story pretty well. This time, there're more wacky details about Sasha's dad being clueless. I appreciate Liam's artistic freedom.

Armand, the red-haired social worker who's in charge of the youth section of the LGBT+ Center, shows up right in time to hear the story's punchline.

"They thought my bag was a bomb!!"

Armand shouts, "A bomb?!"

"Yes! Then I got emotional. I was so scared that I might have lost my bag, and I was so glad it was still there and that the NYPD didn't have time to blow it up yet, and I started crying tears of joy, it was overwhelming. That's when I wanted to give the police officer a hug, but he just yelled 'Step back!' and went to reach for his gun. Can you imagine?"

"What the heck? But hey, sorry to interrupt you folks, I just wanted to tell you the food is ready, help yourself when you want."

"Awesome! Thanks."

"Also, Liam, I'm very happy you made it back alive and that you're here with us tonight."

"Aww, thank you, Armand. Anyway, I still managed to grab a selfie with the policeman, look at his face...."

"Ha ha ha! He looks so grumpy."

Liam puts his phone away, and we get in line for the buffet table. Tonight, it's pizza and different types of pastas, sauces, salads, and breads. Every week, a different restaurant from the Village volunteers to prepare the meal. It's generous of them. My dad doesn't struggle to feed me, but I know that's not the case for several kids who attend the meetings.

I fill my plate with spaghetti and put some butter on it, which earns me Liam's judgmental look. "Seriously? No sauce, no meat?"

"Sorry, Daddy! I'll get some salad."

"You need protein! And don't call me Daddy: it's weird."

"Is 'Parental Figure' better?"

"Just 'PF' will work."

"Anyway, I think there's protein in butter."

Liam sighs and we sit in a circle with the others, waiting for the more official part of the meeting to start. Nothing complicated: we introduce ourselves and the pronouns we use, it's the same thing every week. Then we're invited to socialize. Sometimes, people leave to go to free concerts downtown as a group or join environmental protests or demonstrations for animal rights or stuff like that. Last week, a bunch of people went to the Museum of Fine Arts just because it's free on Wednesday evenings. But Liam is usually too exhausted to do anything that requires too much energy, which I don't blame him for, considering his intense schedule.

We stay for an hour and a half more, until the place starts emptying out. Armand and a volunteer put the leftovers from the meal in recycled containers and distribute them to anyone who needs them. We're still chatting with Nathan when he stretches his big arms and yawns. "I'm sorry, I need to go now unless I want to catch the last bus at midnight."

"Yeah, we should head out too. I bet Liam is completely pooped."

"Pretty much."

We say good-bye to the staff and as we leave, Nathan takes a couple of free condoms from a basket near the door. I say, "What do you need those for? You didn't mention any new partner!"

"Meh. You never know! Might come in handy."

He's right, and I take some as well. I ask Liam if he needs any, but he shakes his head. "They should put some vaginal ones in there as well. That's not very inclusive."

Nathan frowns. "I actually had no idea they had vaginal condoms."

"What do they teach you at school?"

"Oh dear, don't get me started on that."

But it's too late, Nathan goes on about how terrible sex education is at his school while we walk to Beaudry station. When we're past the subway entrance, he keeps us upstairs because we're going in a different direction from him, and he still has so many curricular flaws to address. When he hears a train arriving at the station, he starts running to the platform and yells, "Can't miss that one! I think I'll post about that whole sex-ed mess on Twitter. Good night!"

"We'll retweet it. Take care!"

"See you soon!"

Turns out it was Liam's and my train, which we've missed. We wave at Nathan, confused and out of breath, from the other side of the platform. He yells again. "Anyway, I also wanted to tell you all the crappy lies my teacher said about HIV. You won't believe me!"

★ ★ ★

Liam gets off at the same station as me, two stops before the one where he lives. It's becoming a habit. He doesn't like the idea of letting me walk home or take the bus late at night by myself. He asks, "Do you want to walk through the park?"

"That'd be nice."

But knowing Liam, I know it's because he's scared for me. Isn't he the sweetest? Seriously.

It's already dark outside, even though it's not even 9 p.m. Besides the inclined Olympic tower behind us, we only get a dim light from the Halloween decorations the doctors who work at the Rosemont hospital have started putting on their cozy detached houses, on Viau street. There's a thin lunar crescent. Liam bends down and picks up a leaf. He looks at it closely and twirls it between his fingers, pointing at a tree in front of us. "Can you hear it? That tree. It goes 'tshh, tshh.'"

"Yeah, it's the wind."

"No, but listen carefully. It's louder than the other trees."

I pause for a moment. Liam shows me the leaf. "It's called a 'tremble.' Some kind of poplar tree. It has very hard, round, thick leaves. That's why when the wind hits them, they make such loud noises. It's like they're shivering."

"They tremble."

We keep walking on the path that leads to my apartment. I ask Liam, "How come you know stuff about trees, now?"

"I've been studying flora for my drawings. I can recognize a dozen types of leaves."

"Useful if we get lost in the woods!"

"No, not really. You can't eat any of the leaves I know. We'll die of hunger way before this knowledge ever comes in handy, I'm sorry."

"What if we meet some enigmatic forest creature who will give us food if we can correctly answer their questions about local flora?"

"Okay, it might help in that one specific situation, I guess."

When we reach the middle of the park, where the lights from the houses and from the inclined tower of the Olympic stadium are at their weakest, we lie down on the grass and look at the stars. There are not too many clouds tonight. I say, "How come you're so talented? I don't get it."

"What do you mean?"

"You do all these cool things. You participate in swimming competitions, you draw, you know cool stuff about trees. You're always so good at everything."

"That's not true. There are tons of things I'm bad at. I just don't put energy into things I don't enjoy, that's why you never see me do, I don't know, tap dancing? I'd be terrible at it."

"Ha ha! Did I ever tell you I took tap dancing classes when I was a kid?"

"Why doesn't that surprise me a single bit?"

"My parents thought it would help me express my creativity, or something. They thought my gender variance might just be a flair for pizzazz."

"I think you definitely also have a flair for pizzazz."

"Oh, thank you. Maybe I do, but I can't dance to save my life. I have no sense of rhythm. You should see how much I struggle in music class."

"I'm sure you have tons of things to be proud of."

"But no real talents! Take Stephie. She's first in the class. A model student. She has one of the best averages in the school. She's a national spelling bee champion."

"What? I never heard that."

"Oops. She made me swear not to tell anyone. She's a bit ashamed of her past."

"Her secret is safe with me."

"And I had lunch with Jayden, today."

"Oh, with the cheerleading squad?"

"Yeah. They invited me to see them perform their routine at the basketball match next week. How cool is that? They've got something going on, you know. I felt bad. What do I do besides being the school's weirdo?"

"It's a hard job, but someone's gotta do it!"

I laugh sarcastically. "Ha. Ha."

Liam tries again. "You excel at being cute…?"

"That doesn't count."

"You're really good at it, though!"

"Stop it!"

I laugh and push Liam lightly on the shoulder. He goes on. "Seriously, though, you're good at cycling. These cycling trips you do with your dad? I don't know many people who can do that."

"That's just…. You just need to cycle for long periods of time."

"And yet, there you are, with that thing that's special to you. I could say the same about swimming or drawing. You do it for a long, long time. That's how anyone develops a skill."

"I'm sure you could do it easily. You're already an athlete."

"We'll have to find out! I'm free next weekend. We should go on a bike trip."

"Deal."

We fist-bump. I'm excited at the prospect of sharing my love for cycling with someone else, especially Liam. I want to start planning our trip right away, but before I can say anything, he says, "I think I want to quit swimming. It's not as fun anymore. Everyone is so competitive. I feel that if I want to keep doing it, I need to sacrifice things I don't want to."

"What would you need to sacrifice?"

"Drawing, for example. But also school."

"I wish I could sacrifice school."

"Not me. I don't like any classes in particular, but it forces me to see people outside of my swimming team and my mom. Helps me get up and eat in the morning. You know I was homeschooled for most of primary? That's what worked best for my training schedule. Also, my mom doesn't believe in the school system. She thinks it indoctrinates children into being soulless robots."

"Lol, your mom is so hardcore."

"She's such a Libra."

"If you say so. But I can't say I disagree with her. I've been bullied enough to know that. Just this morning—"

"What happened?"

"There's these guys who keep harassing me. They pushed me on the stairs."

"Who? I want names."

"I don't know their names; I'm not obsessed like you. One of them has cool hair…."

"Jake? Sullivan?"

"I think it's Sullivan. The other one is always wearing his Montréal hockey cap inside."

"Gabriel."

"That's it. How come you're so good with names?"

"I pay attention, that's all. And I'm gonna kick their butts."

"Don't worry, they're just being annoying. But I wouldn't mind staying home for a bit."

"I totally get that. I sometimes wonder if I'd get bullied too if people at school knew I was trans. But going back to school did help with my depression."

"You had depression? You never told me that."

"I still do. I'm on medication. I was diagnosed a while ago, before I transitioned. I felt like I was a huge disappointment to everyone."

"Hashtag relatable. Did transitioning help?"

"In some ways, of course. It's nicer to be alive."

I take his hand, which has been ripping grass and weeds from the ground. "I'm glad to hear it."

"Hey, look! A shooting star. Make a wish."

I hurry to find something to wish for. The first thing that comes to my mind is that I want a partner to cuddle with. Please please please please. But the shooting star doesn't fade.

"It's a…very long shooting star."

"I think it's actually a satellite."

"Oops."

"Yup. Definitely a satellite."

"Still cool. I say it counts."

We both giggle. I don't want this evening to end, but it's getting pretty cold, and my leggings don't cover my ankles. Liam suddenly turns toward me. "You didn't tell me why you had lunch with the cheerleading squad. You're thinking of joining the team?"

"Believe me, nobody wants that to happen. It would be a catastrophe. No, I was just feeling a bit awkward with Stephie, you know, because of what happened last week. I felt like she was trying to avoid me."

"So, you avoided her."

"I wanted to listen to my horoscope, remember? 'Challenging times, grab every opportunity?'"

"You're not supposed to 'listen to your horoscopes.' They're lenses you can use to analyze your experiences."

"You're speaking gibberish. Anyway, Jayden ended up giving me his phone number. He wants to see me outside of school."

"Oooh, look at you!"

"Hold on, he also said I wasn't his type."

"He can't know that yet. Do you like him?"

"I think he's cute."

"I say go for it."

I add, in the most sarcastic voice I'm capable of, "But I shouldn't think about that, because the Earth's temperatures are rising, and soon we'll all be underwater."

"Are you making fun of me?"

"Maybe...?"

"Climate change and environmental collapse are serious matters. Anyway, we're uphill now, so we're safe."

"Do you think the water could reach the Olympic stadium? Imagine if there was only the tower poking out of the water like a crooked lighthouse."

"We'll have to see, I guess. I hope not, my house is at the bottom of the hill."

We get up and wipe the grass off of ourselves. Time to go home.

"I don't get why we're not preparing for this. Sea levels are rising. We built some of the most powerful dams on the planet for hydroelectricity but won't lift a finger to prevent these disasters from happening."

"Humans are like that. We only understand our hardships after we go through them."

"When it's too late, you mean."

"Yeah. I hope the bookstore will get the book you ordered before the Big Flood."

CHAPTER 7

STEPHIE IS ALREADY at our locker when I get to school the next day. She's wearing mascara and eyeliner again, but this time, no trace of our special lip gloss. When she sees me, she goes, "Hey!"

"Hey. What's up?"

"Nothing much. How was your evening?"

"I went to the youth meeting with Liam. It was nice."

"What did they serve?"

"Pasta."

"Boring."

"No, it was good. There was even garlic bread made with some kind of pizza dough."

"Yeah, you would like that."

"How was your evening?"

"I babysat until late, the parents came back at like, midnight...."

"Midnight? You really don't live by any rules anymore! Such a rebel, oh my God."

She laughs and steps away to let me use the locker. She stays there a moment, holding her books and her pink portfolio with both her arms, not knowing what to say. She breaks the silence. "Did you start writing your book report yet?"

"I don't have time for that!"

"Oh, of course. I forgot you have all these...*things* to do."

"Yeah. All the things. All of them."

"I'm just saying, you won't remember what mine said if you take too long."

I sigh. "I guess you're right."

"I'm always right. I'm also the nicest."

She opens her pink portfolio and hands me a wrinkled document. I read the title: *Kamouraska, creating meaning through confession.*

"That's your book report!"

"That's the copy you ruined with your butt. I figured you'd need it. Don't let anyone see it!"

I squeeze her with all my strength, and I have to stop myself from kissing her neck and her cheek. How can she be so great?

"Don't be so happy! It's a poisonous gift. Now, it'll be harder for you to make it seem like you're not just copying me."

"You can count on me!"

I hide the book report in my school bag and close the locker. Stephie and I walk to French class in silence. I'm struggling to find things I could tell her. My father's girlfriend, who wanted to celebrate Thanksgiving with us even though we've never celebrated it? Weird. Yesterday's shooting star that ended up being a satellite. Silly. The dream I had where my brother was driving a van full of kittens that he was trying to smuggle into the United States? Uninteresting. Or was it? What could it mean?

Then I remember I haven't told her about my date with Jayden, tonight. That's a hard one. I'm scared she might get jealous that I'm seeing him, but that's nonsense because first, it's not a romantic date, despite what everyone seems to believe, and second, Stephie said she didn't want to date me right now. Not wanting to tell her about Jayden has probably more to do with the fact that I don't want her to think I'm not interested in *her*. So, I don't say anything.

We arrive at our classroom and wave at each other. She goes to sit with her friends near the windows, and I sit next to Liam, busy with a drawing. He says, without looking at me, "Hello, lovely water spirit."

"That's me!"

"How are you?"

"Good. I had the wackiest dream. My brother was smuggling kittens into the United States in some stolen van, and I was in the back, and at some point, there was an ambush by bandits who wanted to steal the kittens."

"Did you save them?"

"I'm not sure, it's blurry. I know I escaped the ambush, but then I found a small cabin in the woods and there was a lady I knew in it...."

"Do I know that lady?"

"No. Me neither. But in my dream, I did. Anyway, we had hot chocolate together. What does that mean?"

"That means you had too much pasta with butter yesterday."

"It was really good, okay? But I'm surprised you don't know anything about dream interpretation. Isn't it along the same lines as astrology?"

"I just never got interested in it. I forget all my dreams as soon as I wake up."

"Oh yeah, you told me."

Liam goes back to his drawing for a moment. It's some manga character striking a pose. The second bell rings and class is supposed to start, but Ms. Campeau still looks busy on her laptop, and everyone keeps talking. Liam asks, "So, what do we do this weekend? Is that cycling trip happening?"

"Right! You really want to do it?"

"We fist-bumped it, of course! But it has to be easy. Don't forget I'm a beginner."

"Do you have a place in mind?"

"How about we just cycle until we're tired, and come back?"

"I'd rather not. If we cycle until we're tired...we'll be too tired to come back. It's better if we have a goal, even if we change it halfway. We'll feel more accomplished."

"True that. What kind of goal?"

"A place you want to see, a sight, a monument, a river, anything."

"A family member?"

"Of course!"

Ms. Campeau gets up and closes the door. That means she's ready to start. Silence spreads and she thanks the one student who already gave her their book report, urging others to do the same. I look at Stephie, just to see the face she makes when she's being complimented but doesn't want her pride to show too much. When she does it, she stops moving, pinches her lips, and tries to keep her back as straight as possible. I think it's naive of her. Everyone must know she's the best by now.

A dozen minutes into the lesson, Liam slides a piece of paper onto my desk. It's a drawing of a van full of kittens. On the driver's seat, I recognize my brother from his messy black hair and his large front teeth. The caption says, "direction: USA!" while he's about to crash into a tree. I have trouble not laughing too loudly.

★ ★ ★

"I heard that they put him in jail."

"They can't put him in jail without a trial. We don't even know for sure if he's the one who sent the email."

"Also, they can't put him in jail, because he's like what, ten?"

"He's fifteen, Naomi."

"Well, the police are involved for sure, that's all I know. My brother's friend is on a soccer team that often plays against his, they've been talking about it."

"You got it wrong. He's just expelled. One of his friends told my teacher this morning. He wasn't there."

"Expelled because he's waiting for his trial."

Everybody is talking about Viktor and the leaked pictures again this morning. Neither he nor Raquel are at school today, and the rumors are getting intense. I try to say something interesting. "I know his BFF, he's in one of my classes this afternoon. I'll ask him. He probably knows what's actually happening."

Jayden turns toward me and asks, "Who is it? Mickey?"

"No. Frank."

"Right. They sit together in Science and Techno."

"That's why I was trying to avoid them, last time. I usually sit right behind their table."

"So, you didn't just sit with us because you thought we were cooler? I'm disappointed."

Caroline says that with the heaviest snobby accent she can, and I believe she is sincere for a second, and I turn red. I probably look worried because she starts laughing.

"You're adorable!"

Cynthia defends me. "And you, you're mean! Look at him, he's feeling bad now."

"Them."

"What?"

I explain. "'Look at them.' I'm not a 'he.'"

"Oh! Sorry."

"No worries. I only correct people I care about."

My three classmates all go "aww."

Once lunch is over, we split to go to our lockers. All three of us are going to Science and Techno next. Cynthia asks me, "Alex! Are you sitting with us again?"

"Sure, if you don't mind."

"Not at all, you're welcome! Especially if your other option is near Viktor's BFF...brrr."

I skip to my locker. I must have missed Stephie because she is nowhere to be seen. Then I climb the stairs to the floor where the classroom is and rejoin my new friends, already sitting at their usual spot but reorganized: this time, the two girls are sitting together, and Jayden is sitting by himself. From the way Cynthia and Caroline look at me pulling out the chair, I can tell it's all part of their evil plan to make Jaydex happen.

As the rumors foretold, Frank is alone at his table. I figure the best time to talk to him is at the end of class, even if I'm getting curious and I have so many questions for him. While everyone around us seems busy discussing the last homework, Jayden whispers to me, "Hey, are we still on for tonight?"

"Of course we are! Your place or mine?"

He shrugs and mumbles, "My place is fine."

"Sure! Anyway, my brother can be annoying sometimes."

"I have an older sister who's annoying too, but she works in the evenings. After dinner?"

"I guess. Where do you live?"

"Bellechasse and Saint Michel."

"Nice. That's like, ten minutes by bicycle."

Jayden smiles and it's so luminous that I realize I've never seen him genuinely smile like that before. It changes his whole face.

"You still use your bike? It's almost winter!"

"As long as there's no snow, it's good. No, wait, even with the snow, I don't mind."

He flaps his hand toward me and adds, "You're so funny."

Suddenly our whole table shakes. I look to my left. It's that guy with cool hair, Sullivan, who just doesn't give a shit and bumps into everything he considers in his way. "What a jerk." Jayden sounds fed up.

I whisper, "I think he's targeting me. He and his friends keep bumping into me and throwing me insults."

"They're probably in love with you."

"All of them, at the same time?"

"Heck, imagine the drama! Being stuck in a giant love triangle with the class bullies!"

"A love pentagon!"

"It's something I heard, though. When guys can't process their emotions, they just address everything with anger. Emotional poverty, it's called. Internalized homophobia."

"It's so cliché, though."

"That cliché must come from somewhere, don't you think?"

I take a peek at Gabriel, Sullivan, and the others at the back of the classroom. They sure do look like they can't properly process their feelings. At the same time, I don't want to be the one to help them figure it out. They terrify me.

After class, I tell Jayden, Cynthia, and Caroline to go without me. I head toward Frank's table. He's slowly filling his backpack with his scattered pens and pencils—he doesn't own a pencil case, Stephie told me.

"Hey, Frank."

"Ciel! How are you?"

"Okay. You?"

"I don't know. Things are messed up. You probably heard. Huh…. How's Stephie?"

I think about how she tries to look like she's over him. It would be a bad idea to tell him otherwise.

"She's fine."

"She won't talk to me. She's not answering her phone, and she blocked me on TikTok and Discord. I feel awful. I tried to talk to her in math, but she just went away, so I didn't insist."

"Good call. Give her time."

"I know you're her best friend, so I know which side you're on, but if you could tell her I'm really sorry, that would be nice."

If he only knew how much I hope they never get back together….

"I'll see what I can do."

"You're so sweet. I hope…I hope we're still friends."

I look at him with my poker face. His eyes are asking me for forgiveness. I actually don't think he's so bad.

"It depends. You're still talking to Viktor?"

"Well, you know…it's complicated."

I stare at him.

"I have some yelling to do at him, that's for sure. You want to know what happened yesterday?"

Our teacher, Mr. Brazeau, coughs to get our attention. I suddenly notice we're the only students left in his classroom. He says, with his rusty voice, "Do you have any questions for me?"

"No, sir, sorry. We'll be quick."

"Oh, take your time. I just need to run to the washroom. Close the door when you leave."

Our teacher literally sprints across the school hall. Frank shakes his head. "We're not even allowed to run in the hallways."

"Sometimes people do things they aren't allowed."

I'm surprised at how impetuous that sounded, but it hit where it hurts. Frank loses all his defenses and gets closer to me, as if he wants to tell me a secret. I can now see how red his eyes are, and he splutters, "You have no idea how deep in the shit Viktor put me and everyone else on our soccer team. The police came to my house last night. The police! They wanted to search my phone for the pictures. My mom was crying."

A tear rolls down Frank's cheek. He's dead serious.

"Did they find them? The pictures?"

"I deleted them over the weekend, after Stephie got mad at me."

I breathe again.

"Good."

"But they went to see Mickey and Didier before me. They still had them. They could get a criminal record for possession of juvenile pornography, and they'll have to go on trial with Viktor. I was just lucky. It could have been me!"

I stare at him, feeling dizzy.

"You can't tell anyone at school yet. I think only the principal knows right now. I'd be in trouble if you told anyone."

"Did they find who sent the email?"

Frank shakes his head.

"No clue. Not that I know of."

Mr. Brazeau comes back to the classroom and seems surprised that we're still there. He goes behind his desk without saying anything. The first bell rings. Frank wipes his face with his sleeve and picks up his bag. We mutter "good-bye" to the teacher. Before we go our separate ways, Frank says to me, "Tell Stephie I'm sorry. Please!"

★ ★ ★

The discussion I had with Frank troubles me more than I can bear, and I have to excuse myself to the bathroom twice during my last class. I've known Frank since we were little kids, and the gravity of this whole story upsets me. Why couldn't they all stay out of trouble? Why did Viktor have to show Raquel's pictures around? Because "boys will be boys," so they shouldn't be held accountable for their actions? Now the entire school is a minefield, Raquel's dignity will probably be set against these boys' futures and reputations, and it makes my anxiety peak, even though I have nothing to do with it. I don't even want to think about what it must be like for Raquel.

I finally get to go home, after seeing Stephie at the locker and wishing her a fun evening. It's her night out with her mom. Every other week, they go see a show together, usually a play, but sometimes fancy stuff like the opera or ballet. It always sounds wonderful and nerdy. They invited me a couple of times, out of pity because I don't have a mom to do those things with, but it doesn't happen anymore, probably because Stephie spends less time at home with her babysitting job and they need quality mother-daughter time by themselves. I get that.

I'm so overwhelmed by the situation at school that I almost forget I'm supposed to meet Jayden after dinner. Once I'm done setting the table—I earned that responsibility for the rest of my life after my fancy-napkin-folding phase—I text him for his address. He gives it to me and writes,

We're eating in like 30 minutes, so in an hour would be perfect.

Should I be scared of your parents?

Trick question. Maybe? Be polite and say hi to them, but don't discuss too much. They might try to make terrible jokes.

That's good advice!

They usually watch TV after dinner, so you might not even see them.

My dad cooked an entire chicken with potatoes and tomatoes. That's his specialty, in my humble opinion. With the leftovers, he'll make a sandwich mix that we'll get in our lunches tomorrow. I debate whether or not I should bring up what Frank told me. Virgil is there, sharing every little detail of his day at school. He's very receptive to drama (it kind of amuses me), but I don't want him to start worrying about that. Once he's done rambling, my dad turns to me and asks how my day was. I bite my lower lip and try to come up with something that's true but not the whole truth at the same time. "Um, there's this guy at school who shared naked pictures of his girlfriend with some boys."

"Without her underwear?"

"Yes, Virgil, that's what naked means."

My dad stays serious. "You told me about that."

"Yeah, but now the whole school knows, so it's very tense."

My dad sighs and wipes his eyes. "I hope this girl is holding up okay. Do you know her?"

"A little. She's always been mean to Stephie and me. A bit of a transphobe."

My brother plays with his food and whispers, "Naaakeeeed."

I add, "Apparently, the police are involved."

"I believe there should be consequences."

"Yeah. Oh, and I'm seeing a new friend tonight."

"What's their name?"

"Jayden. He uses 'he/him/his.'"

"Have I met him before?"

"I only told you about him. He's the gay kid in my class."

"Oooh, is that the one you said was too cool for you?"

"Ha ha. Yeah, maybe!"

We finish eating and when all the dishes are in the dishwasher, I retreat to my bedroom to change before heading to Jayden's house. I'm a bit scared of his parents. What if they don't like me? I shouldn't be wearing anything too flashy or colorful. I have no idea what Jayden told them about me. What if he said I was a boy? I don't feel like explaining my gender to Jayden's parents. He already felt so uneasy when I asked him about them, I don't want to find out why.

I settle for a white dress shirt and skinny jeans. I check my hair one last time and text Jayden:

I'm on my way.

The address he gave me is a brown block that looks more stylish than the one where I live. You have to go inside and call the person you're visiting to get them to open the second glass door. When I call the number for Jayden's apartment, he answers very quickly, as if he had been waiting nearby. His voice sings,

"Hello!"

"Hey, it's Alex."

"Come on in. It's on the third floor. I'll wait outside."

A loud buzzing sounds makes me jump back. My dad always says I'm a scaredy-cat, but I just get startled whenever

I hear a sound I wasn't expecting. I open the glass door and climb the numerous little flights of stairs to the third floor. I spot Jayden in a corner, busy on his phone, leaning by a door. When he sees me, he puts his phone in the back pocket of his yoga pants and says, "You made it!"

"I know. Impressive, right?"

He invites me in. The first thing I notice is the huge blue-white-red Acadian flag hanging on the wall, over a display of maritime paraphernalia: a miniature lobster cage, the model of a boat, a clam plush toy holding another tiny Acadian flag…. When Jayden sees that I'm interested in his parent's tastes in interior design, he gets a desperate look on his face and instructs me to hang my jacket on a hook near the door.

The apartment is bigger than you'd think from the out-side. It's as long as the building and seems to have windows on every wall. At one end of the hall, where the entrance is, there's a kitchen with a balcony, and right next to it, a dining room with a TV.

"You mean you don't eat right in the kitchen? That's so posh!"

Although it isn't luxuriously decorated or anything, I can't help but be impressed at how spacious it feels. My family's apartment is so small in comparison. Jayden laughs nervously. He doesn't think much of the whole thing.

"Here's the washroom. Over there, that's the living room, but my parents are watching their show right now…."

They don't seem to have noticed us because their eyes are absorbed by the screen. I catch a glimpse of them: his father looks like a balder, larger, and less sassy version of him, while his mom is tall and thin with sharp facial features. I point at a door, behind the television. "Wait, is that another balcony?"

"Yes, we have two."

"This place is like a palace!"

"Stop saying that! This place sucks. There's rats in the walls."

"Rats? That's awesome! One of my friends had one, they're so cute."

"I meant mice. And you're weird. Here's my bedroom."

Jayden closes the door behind me. His room is painted navy blue and has a window covered outside by a tree. I bet he can hear birds sing in the morning. He has a PC with a large black screen decorated with photo-booth pictures of Cynthia, Caroline, and him. On his dresser, there's a framed picture of a kid in a sparkly spandex costume hanging from a bar. "Is that you?"

"Yeah. Back when I was doing gymnastics."

"That is the cutest thing."

"I didn't really like it. It was stressful. Cheerleading is a lot more fun."

"Did you do competitions?"

"Only once, something really low key. I think that's when the picture was taken, I don't remember. We mostly just practiced and did terrible shows in front of the parents. I have some videos somewhere if you ever need to blackmail me!"

"Duly noted. I have videos too, from when I was doing tap dancing."

Jayden starts laughing with that shining smile that spreads across his whole face. I can't help but chuckle too. He says, "Okay, that is *so* gay."

I can't believe my ears. "You're the one saying that? I was wearing top hats and bow ties while you were twirling ribbons in a spangly bodysuit!"

"You've got a point. Oh, I think I still have it somewhere!"

Jayden opens his spacious wardrobe and searches very deep inside it. He emerges victorious with the tiny costume he was wearing in the picture.

"It's so small! Do you still fit in it?"

"Oof, I wouldn't try. I was, like, nine when I wore it. It's very stretchy, though."

He throws the costume on the pile of clothes in his wardrobe. I sit on his bed and say, "I wish I had known someone like you when I was nine."

He looks at me briefly. Maybe that was too personal? Or too direct? We were having fun, why did I have to ruin everything with my feelings? He's smiling at me in silence. It's awkward. I made it awkward. So, I make it worse. "It would have felt less lonely."

"Yeah. Same."

Suddenly, there are so many things I want to ask him. I want to know every aspect of our lives that we might have in common. Was he bullied in elementary school? Did adults make him feel like he was to blame for it because he wasn't behaving in typical masculine ways? Did he try to conceal his gender expression? Did he feel like he was playing a role, to the point of not being entirely sure who he actually was? How annoying is his sibling? I want to know everything, but I ask, "What did you want to talk about?"

He sits on his computer chair and puts his feet on the bed next to me.

"Nothing in particular, more like…different little things."

"Like what?"

"Well, the other day at school, we talked about how I'm not out to my parents. I've been thinking about it. How did it go for you?"

"It went well, in general. I came out several times."

"How come?"

"Well, as different things. I came out as gay when I was seven, then I came out as non-binary five years ago, then I came out as a non-binary girl three years ago, and as bisexual last week…."

"And your dad was alright with all that? How did you do it? Did you just…tell him, bam, just like that?"

"Basically, yes. But it's a bit more complicated. I was just never…not out. I never felt like I needed to be closeted about anything with my parents."

"You're lucky. I don't think I could ever do that. I don't talk to my parents that much. I get nervous just thinking about it."

"I know it's a weird thing to say, but they probably at least suspect you're not a cis, straight guy."

"Yeah but it's hard to get to the bottom of things with them. As soon as I try to discuss serious matters, they act as if it wasn't a big deal and pretend that all is well. But all is not well, and this is a big deal for me. My worst nightmare is that they'll just shrug their shoulders and say 'yeah, we knew that, old news' and turn up the volume on the TV."

I think for a moment. "You could write a letter and ask them to read it in front of you. They wouldn't be able to shut down a discussion, and you'll be able to tell them everything you want."

"I've thought about that. That might be the best idea."

"I can help you with the letter if you want. Well, not writing it, because I suck at that, but I can give you feedback if you write one."

"That's very nice. Thank you."

"No problem. I'm glad you asked, seriously."

Our legs are touching on the bed. I actually feel useful, for once. We stay like that for some very long seconds, until Jayden gets up and asks, "Do you want something to drink? There's juice, coke, milk, almond milk...."

"Ooh! Almond milk. Fancy. I'll have that."

Jayden laughs at my reaction and repeats "fancy" as he leaves me alone in his room. I wonder if something could happen between us. Maybe not something deep, like being partners, that would be a tad unrealistic, but just experimenting together. Not being very close friends could turn out to be useful, since there would be fewer consequences. How do I bring that up?

He comes back with two glasses and a box of Celebration cookies, the ones with dark chocolate on top of shortbread biscuits. He hands me the almond milk and takes a big gulp from his glass of coke before opening the cookie box.

"Want some?"

"These are so good; I'll have to refrain from eating the whole package."

"I won't let you, don't worry!"

We munch and sip for a little while. Jayden looks at some notifications on his phone. When he puts it back in his pocket, I do a power move. "Did I mention the LGBT+ Youth group is having a Halloween party next week?"

"I think you did. Why?"

"We should go together. It'll be fun!"

"Yeah, I could probably convince my parents to let me go to a Halloween party. Okay. We have a date!"

He probably says a lot of things after that, but the word "date" just dances in my mind until I fall asleep in my own bed, two hours later.

CHAPTER 8

THE COLD, autumn rain is pouring when I head out in the morning. I can't even see Maisonneuve Park on the other side of the street. I usually wear the same running shoes, whether it rains or not (my rubber boots are so ugly that I'm ashamed to be seen in them), but today is so bad that it would completely ruin them. The boots are dark khaki green, have a suspicious moldy smell, and can't be matched with anything. I wish I had stylish ones like Stephie. Hers are scarlet red with black dots. I could wear them even when it's not raining.

I woke up thinking about Jayden. I wanted to text him as soon as I opened my eyes, two minutes before my alarm, but couldn't find anything to tell him. I usually text Stephie first thing in the morning. Of course, I didn't want to spill anything about my date with Jayden, so I just sent her a GIF of a sleepy cat. She replied with a GIF of the sun saying "good morning," but that's all.

On my way to school, I start thinking about what it would be like to date Jayden. Maybe it would stop being awkward between Stephie and me if I was with someone else? That thought makes me happy, and I skip on the sidewalk. Nobody can see me with that thick rain curtain anyway.

I remember the discussion I had with Frank yesterday. I guess I'll have to tell Stephie how sorry he is. After what he said, I would feel like a first-class a-hole if I didn't. I don't know when a good time would be to tell her, though. I don't really see myself coming up to her and going like, "Hey princess"—I call her princess when I want to tease her, and she frowns but she likes it—"I know we've barely talked this week, but I spoke to your awful ex, and he says he's sorry." That'd be weird.

There are so many things I wish I could tell her. I just don't know how to. We never fight, and it's the first time we've gone through such intense drama. Are we supposed to just wait and stare at each other silently at the locker until we both forget why we're feeling like this? That's what we've always done for minor issues, like that time she mistakenly put my mom's scarf in her school bag, and I spent days looking for it but it was in her dad's living room. Or when I gave her my yogurt at lunch, but it was curdled and she got so sick that she had to miss school and a spelling contest the next day. It wasn't even my fault.

Yesterday evening has given me an idea. I could write a

letter to Stephie, just like Jayden wants to do to come out to his parents. It would give me a chance to tell her everything without changing my mind halfway through. Last year, we wrote each other letters over a couple of weeks. It was nice, but I'm not thinking of reviving that dead tradition unless she wants to. This is more of a one-time thing.

I arrive at school a bit late. I guess the first bell has already rung because people are moving toward their classrooms. I walk faster and my ugly boots make tons of insufferable sharp sounds. It's a relief to take them off at the locker. My socks got a bit wet but they're not too bad. Stephie's red rubbers are already there, of course. I feel like trying them on—they're so pretty and I have smaller feet than Stephie—but there's no time for that. I throw my boots on my shelf and hurry to get my shoes out and put them on without tying them.

I race up the stairs to French class. Liam is already there, the privilege he gets from living nearby. He says, "Wow, you're on time! Congratulations."

"Oh, stop it. I haven't been late in two weeks."

There's still half a dozen students missing. Buses must be running late. I spot Stephie in a corner, but she's reading, and I can't make eye contact. Liam goes on, "It better not rain like this the entire weekend."

"Why? Do you have something planned?"

Liam looks at me with big eyes and opens his hands as if he's totally outraged.

"We're going on a cycling trip!"

"Ooooh! I completely forgot."

"Are we still on?"

"Yeah, of course. I'm sorry, there's been a lot on my mind lately."

"I can see that. You never replied to my text yesterday."

"You sent me something?"

I open my phone and go to my message inbox. There it is, sent at 9:17 p.m. I must have opened my phone without reading Liam's message, and the notification disappeared.

"I was with Jayden…."

"I figured. How was it?"

"Good. We, uh…we're going on a date. To the Halloween party next week."

"The one at the LGBT+ Center? You're supposed to bring a date? Oh no!"

"No, no, it's just me, I asked him to come. What was your message about?"

"I just wanted to discuss that cycling trip. I think I have an idea for where we could go."

"Go on."

"There's my aunt Constance, who lives in Repentigny, on the North Shore. I checked on Google maps, and it says that the round trip by bicycle is four hours. I think I could do that, with enough breaks!"

"That's a good idea. She's nice?"

"Yeah. She's my godmother. She's hilarious."

The second bell rings and Ms. Campeau goes to close the door when three students arrive *in extremis*. They're soaking wet and their hair is dripping. Our teacher gives them a chance to sit down before starting her lesson. I whisper to Liam, "I need to write a letter. Do you have any nice paper?"

"A letter to who? Jayden?"

Liam flaps his eyelashes and reaches for his sketchbook in his bag.

"It's actually for Stephie."

"I see. Would this work?"

He opens the sketchbook on a page covered in light watercolors.

"I meant blank paper. But that's beautiful!"

Liam rips the sheet from the book and hands it to me.

"I did that in ten seconds with large brushes. It's meant to be written on."

"Thanks!"

I open my French notebook and pretend I'm taking notes, but I write in the same style as last year, when Stephie and I were exchanging letters in class.

Hello my beloved wolverine,

I hope the harvest has been good and the blood moon shed its light on your clan in the most beneficial manner. Over here, the promise of winter has already taken a toll on our spirits. I miss laughing with you. I wish things could be like before, and I'm sorry if I did anything I shouldn't have done.

I heard your cow has given birth. At least, that's something to celebrate. I hope you'll name the calf after me.

Yours Truly,
Ciel

The result is quite satisfying. There's enough space at the bottom to draw a picture, so I sketch a cow giving birth but it ends up being very scary. It's perfect.

I show it to Liam, who smiles when he sees the cow. He gives me a thumbs-up. I fold the letter and try to focus on the rest of the class while wondering when the best moment would be to give it to Stephie. Right now wouldn't be ideal, since she would probably have time to read it before lunch, but not enough time to write a reply, and we will probably bump into each other at some point, and it would be embarrassing and all. The best would be to put it in her school bag in the afternoon, so she will read it when she gets home.

My plan is almost wrecked when class is over. Stephie stops by my desk, and I almost instinctively hand her the letter. I must resist. Liam, Stephie, and I start walking together. She asks, "How are you?"

"I'm fine. How was the play yesterday?"

Stephie turns her head around. I imitate her. It's Raquel, going in the opposite direction from us. I'm surprised she decided to come back to school so soon. Stephie clears her throat and says, "It was really unsettling. It was experimental theatre. There were lots of lights and strobes…. You wouldn't have liked it. My mom did, though."

"Good for her. Remind me not to go see it."

"I will. It was the stuff of nightmares. What's up, Liam?"

"Not much. We're going on a cycling trip tomorrow."

"A cycling trip? It's gonna be freezing!"

"We know! I can't wait."

"I'm visiting my grandma tomorrow. It should be nice."

"Tell her I said hi!"

I was invited to spend a couple of days at her grand-mother's cottage over the summer. She is a sweet old lady who lives alone near the Appalachian Mountains, by the US border. It's a really pretty place. We had tons of fun there, especially because it was during that awful heatwave, and she has a big swimming pool that we shared with her neighbors.

As we're about to reach the staircase, we hear a loud voice coming from behind. "I can't believe you dare show your face here after Viktor got expelled because of you. Bitch!"

It's Sullivan, with his cool hair and his pack of followers. One of them adds, "It takes some guts, girl! I would watch your back if I were you."

Liam curses and turns around. In three big steps he's near them and he shouts, "You leave her alone, fucker."

Sullivan says with disdain, "What did you call me?"

Stephie stays near the staircase. She looks petrified. I can't leave Liam by himself, so I run over to him.

"Oh, are you that fag's bodyguard?"

Sullivan turns to face Raquel again. "Anyway, welcome back, sweetie pie. You're just making a martyr out of Viktor."

He spits on the floor and pushes Liam with both his hands. Then he signals to his little troop to follow him away, bumping into everyone in their path, including me. I don't care, I'm just relieved that it didn't end in a fight. Gabriel, still wearing his cap inside, looks straight at me and it's really hard not to look back at him.

Once they're out of sight, Stephie comes up to us. She's visibly shocked. I say to Liam, "Hey, what was that?"

"That guy, I hate him so much."

"So do I, but did you seriously think you stood a chance? He wouldn't have hurt Raquel, but I'm not that sure about you."

"I couldn't just walk by. She's dealt with enough."

We look at Raquel, who's surrounded by a couple of her friends trying to comfort her. Liam goes up to the group and asks, "You're alright? You know you can count on us if there's anything. Should we tell the principal?"

Raquel nods and Liam comes back. I don't think I've ever seen him show such bravery. It's kinda hot.

★ ★ ★

I sneak my letter inside Stephie's backpack during the afternoon break. I place it inside her math workbook so it doesn't get crumpled, but let it poke out a bit, so she'll see it without opening the book. When I see her at the locker at the end of the day—I need to take my umbrella and my ugly boots home even if it's not raining anymore, otherwise they will stink on Monday (I learned the hard way)—she's carefully placing her pink portfolio in her bag. She hasn't noticed the letter. I feel so sneaky. We follow each other outside and say good-bye at the bus stop.

I take my phone and earbuds out of the pockets of my raincoat and put on the soundtrack of the *Lafontaine* musical, mostly as a way to avoid interacting with the mass of students walking slowly on the sidewalks. For some reason, they always try to grab my attention, probably precisely because I don't want to give it to them, and I avoid looking in their direction. Most of the time, I don't even know who they are. They might have heard of me through the grapevine. Or they might be blinded by my queerness. Or they might just be nice, I don't know. I'd rather not take any chances since I don't have my bicycle. My bike makes me stronger. I feel protected on it. It enhances my powers. It gives me a means to leave and flee. It gives me confidence.

I finally escape from the hordes of teenagers clogging the streets around the school. The wind is strong and pushes the low-rolling clouds across the sky. The elements hit my face. I'm glad I wrote and gave that letter to Stephie. I can't wait to talk to her once she reads it. And I'm excited to cycle to Repentigny with Liam tomorrow. This weekend will be awesome.

I do a routine check over my shoulder and see a familiar red cap: it's Gabriel from school, walking a couple of meters behind me. My heart starts pounding. What is he doing here?

I don't want to be alone with him, even though he doesn't have anyone to impress right now, since Sullivan isn't around. Maybe it's just a coincidence, maybe he lives nearby. I start walking faster, but he does too. I cross the street. He crosses too. That makes it clear. He's definitely following me.

I take my phone out of my pocket and pretend to dial a number. I put it against my ear, over my earphones. It tricks your stalker into thinking you're calling the police, or someone who could get very angry if they knew you were being harassed. I read that on the Internet. But it doesn't seem to work, he's still behind me. I decide to keep walking and wait until we're at the next street. There are people at the bus stop. I'll confront him there, where it's safer.

When we get there, I start walking slower. I take the earbuds out of my ears, turn around, and yell, "Okay, stop following me! What's your problem?"

Gabriel stares at me. I can't tell if he's surprised or confused. He looks around and seems to notice all the people at the bus stop, who are getting interested in the scene. He whispers, "Hey, it's fine. I just want to talk."

"I don't. Leave me alone. Good-bye."

I stay there and wait for him to go away, but he stays there, with the same numb expression on his face.

"I just…think you're really cute."

Heck, Jayden was right. I can't believe it. Good thing we didn't bet money on this cheesy scenario. I'm torn between being flattered and finding him pathetic. I still want him to leave. I say, "Thank you."

"I'm…I'm…I'm not gay, though. Right? That makes sense?"

I chuckle, trying to repress laughter. "I don't know, you tell me! I can't know for you."

"I just wanted to say, I'm sorry for the things Sullivan does. He's my friend, but…. He doesn't listen."

"Yeah, I got that vibe from him."

"No hard feelings?"

"Whoa, whoa. I was about to call the police on you, man."

"What? Why?"

"You and your friends bully me for weeks and…and you start following me in the street! What did you expect?! I was scared for my life. 'No hard feelings…?'"

"I'm sorry."

"I know. You'd better be sorry."

I stop talking for a moment. I have to calm down. People are lining up to get on the approaching bus. They stopped watching when they understood that nothing bad was going to happen.

I look at Gabriel's face under his Canadiens hockey cap. I never really noticed his features before. He doesn't look so tough when you're near him. He has baby cheeks that are covered in peach fuzz and a small, flat nose, like Borki's nose when he was a puppy. I think I understand what I see in his brown eyes: it's neither surprise nor confusion, it's fear. That boy is terrified of me.

The silence is getting awkward. Gabriel says, "Do you think we could see each other someday?"

I have trouble processing all this information: how Gabriel, out of anyone, is in love with me; how for once when someone has a crush on me, I'm the one who's completely uninterested; and how I'm still gonna go for it.

"Yeah. Okay."

"Can I have your phone number?"

"It's 514...."

Gabriel enters my number in his phone and sends me a message that reads,

hey :)

I show him the screen of my phone so he can see that I received it, and we exchange uneasy smiles. He mutters, "I guess I'll go.... I'll text you."

"Cool. Have a good weekend!"

"You too. Bye!"

He waves shyly as he walks away backward in some attempt to look cool, but he trips on a hole in the sidewalk. When he gets back up, he looks at me and says, "Oh, and please don't tell anyone about any of this."

I sigh. Of course he would say that. This isn't getting less absurd.

"I won't."

CHAPTER 9

I DON'T TELL my dad about my encounter with Gabriel during dinner. Not because Gabriel told me not to tell anyone (yeah right, as if) but out of fear my dad wouldn't approve of me seeing him. I have no clue how I could talk about him without mentioning the bullying and his general grossness. "Oh, he's some guy who always wears a hockey cap inside. He has a puppy nose." Instead, I talk about the letter I wrote to Stephie. Virgil really wants to see the drawing of the cow giving birth, so I promise him to ask Stephie for a picture of it.

Virgil is ecstatic about getting his scout troop to accept the idea of a drag talent show. The meeting is tonight. He's eating with half of his outfit on, his cub shirt off to avoid spilling my dad's spaghetti sauce on it. As soon as he's done (quicker than usual), he excuses himself from the table to finish preparing. My dad asks, "I'm going to do groceries while Virgil is at his meeting. Do you want to come?"

"I'm so tired…."

"It's fine. Need something? Besides…."

"Pistachio ice cream."

"Yeah, besides that."

"Hmmm, those veggie samosas you bought the other time."

"Oh yeah, we liked them. Gotcha."

I clear the table while my dad puts the leftovers away. Once I'm done, I go lie on my bed. I'm playing games on my phone when Stephie messages me:

You're SO SWEET!

She sends a picture of the card I made her.

Did you make the paper? It looks amazing.

It's a page from Liam's sketchbook. Glad you liked it!

The cow is spooky, though.

Ha ha yeah, oops. Do you mind sending me a picture of it? I told Virgil about it and now he wants to see it.

She sends the picture and writes,

Sorry if I seemed distant lately. It's been a rough week.

Yeah, for me too.

Wanna hang out tonight?

Sure. You could come over. My dad and bro are gone for the evening.

On my way!

I show my brother the picture of the cow (he says he's gonna have nightmares about it) and say good luck to him before he leaves with my father and Borki. I ask, "Is it okay if Stephie comes over?"

My father replies, "Of course. If you go out, don't forget to lock the door!"

"I won't! Bye bye."

I crash on the couch and go back and forth on all the apps on my phone while I wait for Stephie. I send a message to Liam to confirm our meeting point tomorrow morning: 10 a.m. at his house. He's not online. He's probably at swim practice. Then I stalk Jayden's Instagram. At lunch today, I subscribed to a bunch of cheerleaders' profiles and got most of them to follow me back, and now my Instagram feed is filled with pictures of older students whose names I can't remember.

Almost every picture Jayden has on there is a selfie taken from a weird angle. There's a couple of them in his cheerleading uniform (they're the cutest) and others with makeup experimentations. I actually had no clue he was into makeup;

I've never noticed him wearing any at school. I'll have to bring that up next time I see him. It could be a fun playdate.

I finally hear steps on the staircase and get up to open the door before Stephie has a chance to knock. She starts complaining as soon as she sees me. "I can't believe it took me so long! I was unlucky with the buses."

"Ha ha! It's fine."

She leaves her shoes on the little mat next to a pile of dog toys. "What have you been up to?"

"Just chilling. Today was exhausting."

"Yeah? You mean that fight in the school hall?"

"Oof, if it was only that…. Take a seat. You'll need it. So, I was walking home from school and I noticed this guy who hangs out with that gang, the one who's always wearing a hockey cap…."

"Gabriel."

"Yeah, him. How come everybody knows everybody else's name? There are hundreds of us. Anyway, he was following me outside. I got so scared, I thought he wanted to beat me up or something."

"What did you do?"

"I waited to reach a bus stop to confront him so there would be people around."

"Oh, cool. Like in that article."

"Yeah. Turns out he just wanted my number."

"What the heck?"

"Exactly. He said he thought I was cute."

"He's not wrong. Did you give it to him?"

I raise my shoulders. The more I talk about it, the more I feel ashamed.

"I did. He looked sincere. I thought 'why not?' Oh, you're going to laugh, though. When he told me that he thought I was cute, he immediately added, 'But I'm not gay!!'"

"Ah ah ah! Oh no! Hashtag save-the-straights. So, are you gonna see him?"

"I don't know. I'm in no rush."

I feel like telling her I want to see how my Halloween date with Jayden goes before planning anything with Gabriel, but she doesn't even know about that. A part of me still hopes we'll end up together, she and I.

"Do you think he's cute?"

"Gabriel? He's…alright, I guess."

"Let's say he asked you out. Would you say yes?"

"Well, it could be fun. Better than nothing."

"That's what I think too. You need a distraction."

"I just don't think he would 'ask me out.' He doesn't want anyone to know he's attracted to me."

"What?!"

"Yeah. Before leaving, he said, dead serious, 'don't tell anyone about any of this.'"

"Ciel! This is bad. That's a red flag. I can't believe it."

"It probably comes from insecurity."

"Still! You can't settle for this. If someone loves you, they should want to celebrate their love, not hide it."

"I agree, but what can I do? We haven't done anything together yet. I'll see."

"If I were you, I would wait before being alone with that guy. Have a first date in public, in a restaurant or a coffee shop. You read that article about safety in public spaces."

"That's probably the best idea, yeah."

"I can even be your chaperone if you need me to. I'll protect you!"

"You're the best."

"No, you're the best."

She hugs me hard enough to make me lose my breath. She smells so good, it's unbelievable. While she's close to me, she says, "I care about you. You're like a sibling to me."

"Aww, that's cute."

My heart is melting, but I'm a bit disappointed: siblings can't be in love with each other. She says, "I don't know what you were planning to do, but I brought some homework...."

"Nah. Homework is bad for our health, I read that somewhere."

"You read more random articles online than the books we're assigned."

"It was in a newspaper."

"How about listening to the soundtrack of *Lafontaine* and painting our nails?"

"That's more like it!"

We move to my bedroom. I connect my small desktop speakers to my phone and open the music player app, which still has the album ready because it's the last thing I listened to on my way home. As the horns from the opening act are blowing, I take the old-fashioned shoe box with all of my nail polishes inside and put it on the bed near Stephie, who gets first pick. She takes the lightest pink I have, of course. She likes them the most. Light pink, almost white.

I find the metallic green she gave me for my last birthday. It's not because I'm deeply in love with her, it's genuinely my favorite color. I think. When she recognizes it, she does that little smile like she's proud of something but doesn't want others to know. But I know. She says, imitating an overexcited little girl, "You're going to look like a mermaid!!"

I reply, with the most high-pitched voice I physically can, "And you, like a princess!!"

We each put a base layer on our own hands before painting each other's, singing along to the musical's songs. At one point, when we're both waiting for our nails to dry and a song that isn't amongst our favorites is playing, I finally gather the courage to tell her, "I talked to your ex the other day."

"Hm hm?"

"He wanted to tell you he's sorry."

"I bet his ass he is. What did you tell him?"

"That he shouldn't expect you to talk to him so soon, especially if he's still talking to Viktor."

"Right on."

"The police went to his house at the beginning of the week to search his phone. Can you imagine?"

Stephie lifts her head up.

"Whoa. Really?"

"They didn't find anything, apparently. He deleted the pictures in time. But Viktor's other friends weren't so lucky. They'll be charged, listen to this, with 'possession of juvenile pornography.'"

"I'm glad they're doing something about it. And good for Frank, I guess."

"Yeah…."

There, it's done. I feel relieved. Now I can cross that off my to-do list: speak-up for my crush's ex-partner…check.

The first act of the show is almost over and the second layer of nail polish practically dry when my dad comes back from the grocery store, making all sorts of noise. He calls my name from the kitchen. I reply, "We're in here."

With his muzzle, Borki opens my bedroom door and comes to say hi to Stephie, followed by my dad. He says, in an exhausted voice, "We won't annoy you too long. I just came back to put the groceries away before the end of your brother's meeting. You probably don't want your ice cream melted! How are you, Stephie?"

"I'm doing great, and you?"

"Not bad. Have you eaten?"

"I did!"

"Just in case, I bought peanut butter cookies. I know you like them. They'll be in the cupboard!"

"Wow, thanks Lucas!"

"No worries. Come, Borki!"

Our dog trots out of the room. I like Borki, but he's messed up my nails too many times for me to feel safe with him around right now. After a couple of minutes, my dad and Borki leave again. Stephie gets up. "I think it's fine now. The polish must be dry."

"Yeah. Let's go get cookies."

★ ★ ★

A box of peanut butter cookies later, my dad, brother, and dog are back. We're about halfway into the second act of *Lafontaine* when my brother erupts into my bedroom, jumping around and yelling, "It got accepted! We're doing a drag talent show!"

Stephie applauds. "That's amazing! Congratulations."

"I even told Bagheera, the troop leader, that you knew a journalist who could talk about it in the papers. We'll need her contact info."

Stephie and I look at each other. She gave him that idea. I don't want to be implicated, even if I do know the journalist Stephie mentioned, Melinda. She works with the *Metro* daily newspaper. I met her during a series of interviews she did about the Youth Committee of the LGBT+ Center. She was nice. She wanted to talk to participants. I don't have her contact information, since it was Armand who organized everything. But Stephie does, from that time a video she put on YouTube against transphobia went viral. She even went on TV to talk about it. She says to Virgil, "I'll find her email address and give it to Ciel."

"Yay! Thank you."

My brother is about to dance his way out of the room when Stephie stops him. "Wait, is Bagheera his real name?"

Virgil raises his shoulders.

"I don't know. Maybe."

CHAPTER 10

STEPHIE ENDS UP leaving at around 9:30 p.m., and I decide to go to bed early so I'm not too tired for the bike ride with Liam the next day, but I have trouble falling asleep. Wrapped up in my blanket, I keep thinking about Gabriel and how creepy my encounter with him was. I open and close his text message on my phone several times, the one that just says "hey :)." I'm afraid of what the next one will be, but I fear my answer even more. Who knows what I'm capable of?

I wake up first, followed closely by Borki, who must have heard my steps on the squeaky wooden kitchen floor. Virgil joins me while I have breakfast. I say, "*Bom dia*" to him, and he just mumbles it back while snoozing in his cereal.

I put on my favorite cycling outfit. It's black and has some kind of robot unicorn design on it. It's so rare that I get to go on long rides with a friend, so it's a special occasion. Then I sneak into the shed in the backyard to fetch my dad's bicycle bag with all the tools and the maps in it. Liam is going to be so impressed. I want him to know he's in safe hands.

Once the bag is secured on the bicycle and my water bottles are washed and filled, I text Liam to tell him I'll be there in thirty minutes. He replies with a terrible selfie of himself on his pillow.

This is what I look like today.

I'm sure your face will change once you see me.

He sends me another selfie of him beaming with joy.

This is what I look like when I think about you.

Aww! I knew it.

I make a couple of sandwiches for both of us (there's some chicken left, but also egg salad, cheese, and pickles) and gather bars and fruit into a plastic bag. I say good-bye to Virgil, put on my bike helmet, and soon, I'm on my way. The air is fresh and there's no sign that it might rain, only big fluffy clouds all over the sky.

The road to Liam's house is almost entirely downhill, so getting there is pretty easy. I even arrive ahead of schedule. He lives in a detached unit at ground level with a ramp for his mom, who sometimes uses a wheelchair. It isn't fancy at all, but the large and heavy copper doorknocker makes it seem like I'm about to enter a gigantic mansion. Each knock vibrates through the walls and through each bone of my upper body, and I can hear Liam's mother tell him to get the door. The first thing he says when he sees me is, "Oh dear! I hope you weren't expecting me to be wearing a cute matching outfit like that."

"Ha ha! I don't, but I'd suggest putting on tighter pants, or else they might get dirty because of your chain."

He lets me in. His place is in a perpetual state of controlled mess: there're piles of stuff everywhere, books and clothes in every corner, and art supplies and art projects abandoned halfway through. They have two cats, Minuit and Glacier, who have shed their hair on every possible surface. The living room is the cats' domain, and it's very rare that we hang out there because it smells a bit like cat pee.

Liam's mom, Sylvie, pops her head out from the kitchen. "Good morning, Alex! So, you're going to go visit my witch of a sister, eh?"

"I guess I am! Should I be scared?"

"I have the feeling she'll like you, so you should be fine. But I wouldn't recommend being alone with her."

Liam takes my hand and drags me into his bedroom. "She's lying! Constance is amazing."

Sylvie yells from the kitchen, "Yeah, when she's not putting curses on your partners!"

Liam tries to find another pair of pants and explains, "That was like, twenty years ago. She cursed my dad. I kind of love her more for that."

"Your whole family is so weird."

126

"Except my dad, actually. He can be so boring. Which might be why my aunt Constance cursed him."

I've never met Liam's dad. I don't even know what he looks like, because Liam has never showed me any pictures of him. He works in a mine in Gaspésie, far down the Saint Lawrence river. Liam only sees him for two weeks in the summer and at Christmas. He sends Liam and his mom a lot of money, but the way Liam talks about him sometimes makes me think he doesn't like him very much.

Liam finds a more suitable pair of sweatpants, much better than the wide jeans he was wearing. He asks me to turn around as he changes, as if I hadn't already seen him half-naked in his swimsuit often enough. Then, we fill his bottles with water, and he shows me his bicycle in the back of the garage that got converted into Sylvie's art studio—that's where she spends most of her days, and there are a number of dishes and coffee mugs lying around. Liam lifts the mountain bike from the ground, ripping apart several spider webs that give a good idea of how much he cares about it. There's a cool-looking, black, cross-country biking helmet hanging on the handles. I press my thumb against the tires and say, "They're a bit deflated."

"Just like my heart."

"Aww. Poor little soul. I have a bike pump in my bag. Let's fix it outside. The tires, not your heart."

Liam carries his bicycle up the ramps until we're on the small patch of pavement in front of the garage door. I ask him to put it upside down while I get the bike pump and a small black bottle from my dad's bag. Liam asks, "What's that?"

"It's oil. We can't remove all the rust from your bike today, but at least it'll roll."

Liam steps back and as I masterfully drop some oil on the chain while pedalling with my hand. When I'm done, I pump some air in the tubes and make sure the wheels are well aligned.

"You can flip it back now."

"Are we ready?"

"Not quite. How long have you had this bike?"

"I don't know. Two years? Three?"

"I bet you haven't adjusted the seat since then. Stand there."

Liam laughs as I unscrew his seat and raise it as high as it can go.

"Wow! That much?"

"Yeah! You're not supposed to hit your chin with your knees when you're pedaling."

"We learn new stuff every day."

We're finally on our way after taking one last, long look at the map on my phone. Repentigny is on the North shore of the Saint Lawrence river, and we get there by crossing a bridge at the easternmost tip of Montréal's island.

"It shouldn't be too complicated. There's a cycling path that follows the river, all the way to Quebec City. It's called the Chemin du Roy, the king's road. We just need to get to Notre-Dame street, and it merges into that old road that basically gets to the sea by following the North shore of the Saint Lawrence river."

"Will we arrive before nighttime?"

"I hope so!! It's not even noon. It's an hour trip to Repentigny."

"An hour for you! You've never cycled with me."

"Come on, it can't be that bad! Let's go."

It's a bit cold for cycling, but Liam makes such good company that I forget about the weather. He always has the wildest anecdotes to tell and an impressive joke repertoire. Good thing there's not many other cyclists in sight, because I just keep laughing while Liam zigzags by my side.

I end up telling him everything I told Stephie about Gabriel the day before. His response is a lot more straightforward than hers. "Ignore him. He's a bully sympathizer. I have no pity for him."

"You can't understand. I'm too insecure to be single. I need the validation."

"No, I do understand. I just think you should be more patient."

Taking time is Liam's motto, which is ironic for a competition swimmer. It was his answer when I asked him out, last year: he wasn't ready. He wasn't in a good place. It's like he's never ready. The complete opposite of Stephie.

That's when it dawns on me: what if Liam has subtly been trying to tell me to wait for him? He's neurotypical like that, he often says things that really mean other things, talking in euphemism and enigmatic allusions. I'm often unsure if he means what he's saying, or if it's sarcasm or irony.

I decide to test his reaction. "You're right, I should wait. I've been hanging with Jayden at school. We have a date next week. I was planning to see how it goes before texting Gabriel back."

"See, dating Jayden would be a much better idea than Gabriel. Plus, he's a lot cuter. I could see you two together."

"So, I have your blessing, Daddy?"

"STOP CALLING ME DADDY!"

I laugh very loudly. Liam pretends to be about to bump into me with his bicycle. He keeps going. "I'm just saying, I get a bad vibe from that Gabriel guy. There's something unsettling about him."

"Yeah, that's what Stephie said as well."

I remain pensive. A part of me is sad that Liam isn't irritated about my dating Jayden, but I'm happy that he thinks we'd make a great couple.

Liam suddenly lifts his head, a stroke of genius in his eyes. "You know what you should do, while we're at my aunt's house? Ask her for a tarot reading! That's her specialty. She's really good at it."

"Tarot? Isn't that a bubble tea flavor?"

"You know what tarot is. The cards. Divination. Cartomancy."

"Oh, of course. Why am I not surprised?"

Most of the road on the way to Repentigny runs through the Bellerive Park, a long patch of trees and grass on the shore of the Saint Lawrence. We stop several times to stretch and drink water before arriving in Pointe-aux-trembles, the last town on the island, named after these noisy trees Liam showed me the other day. We find a picnic table and sit down to eat the sandwiches. After that, we only need to cross the bridge over the Saint Lawrence river to arrive in Repentigny.

At some point, Liam recognizes where we are, and starts giving directions. Soon, we are in front of a century-old stone house, not far from the main road. The grass is long, and there's a big, gray tree that seems to have lost its leaves ages ago. I gasp, "This house is huge! It looks so cool."

"Wait until you see inside!"

Liam rings and in a matter of seconds, a tall old man with thick glasses opens the door and his arms, widely, before inviting us inside. "Hey, Liam! It's been so long. How have you been?"

"I've been good! Eric, this is my friend Alex."

"Hi, good to meet you! Take off your shoes. I'll tell Constance you arrived."

As he walks away, I ask, "Is that your uncle?"

"Yeah, if you want. I just call him Eric. He's been living with my aunt forever. They're both gay and share the house."

The hall is sparingly decorated with art and portraits. I don't have time to study them. Constance arrives and hugs Liam. He calls her, "*God-mama!*"

"I've missed you so much, my dear godson! How long has it been?"

"Since my birthday, I think."

"And you're Alex? Pleased to meet you."

I shake her hand. Maybe it's because Liam's mom called her a witch, but I imagined her dressed all in black with amulets hanging on her neck and sleeping bats on her shoulders.

But, she looks really nice, with her pink shirt and lush, curly black hair. Her hand is soft.

She takes us to the living room, which already has a more New Age feel to it. As she inquires how the trip went and Liam tells her how hard and intense it was, I inspect the room. There are tons of books everywhere, herbs drying here and there, crystals spreading their energy. You can tell this room's purpose is to shake up your senses.

"Have you eaten? I have some quinoa left in the fridge if you want."

"We did! Alex made us an awesome lunch."

I blush. "It was just sandwiches."

"They were perfect."

Liam turns to his aunt and tells her, like a secret, "Alex is a Taurus."

Constance goes "*Oh*," as if everything about me suddenly made sense. Liam continues, "Oh, God-mama, do you think you could give Alex a tarot reading? I told you you were the best at it!"

To which I add, "That's okay too, if you say no. I don't want to bother you...."

Constance laughs and taps her leg. "Of course, I can! It would be a pleasure. Let's go to my office."

She gets up and leads us to the first floor, after climbing some very ancient and narrow stairs over an even older-looking furnace. After passing two bedrooms, we arrive at what must be Constance's office. Liam asks me, "Should I wait outside? I don't mind giving you privacy."

I frown at him and whisper, "I'd rather you stay, please. I'm a bit scared."

He grins and we follow Constance into the room. She sits behind a dark desk covered with a map of the stars. There are posters with diagrams and astrology-related stuff on every wall, and many plants by the window. Dozens of candles are waiting to be lit on a small table. Near the door, a fancy couch with flower patterns must have had better days.

"Bring that couch closer, so you can both sit by the desk. Have you ever had a reading before, Alex?"

"Nope."

"Alright. You see that table with the candles? There's a shelf under it, on which you'll see different little packages. I'm going to ask you to pick one."

"Any one?"

"The one you feel drawn to."

I look under the table. There are maybe eight different packages, each the size of a pound of butter, wrapped in satin cloths. *The one I feel drawn to.* I can't help but find this whole thing silly. I pick one in the middle and put it on the desk. When Constance sees which one I chose, she just nods. Carefully, she unties the satin cloth and reveals a deck of tarot cards.

"This is a deck I received as a gift, a couple of months ago, for another reading I did. It's the newest one I have. Nobody ever chooses it, and it isn't charged with any energy when I try to use it on myself. It's a very special choice. I've never actually used it before."

I smile, thinking she says things like that to everyone. I know how that works.

She puts the deck of cards on her lap and arranges the square piece of satin on the desk before shuffling the cards. With piercing eyes, she asks me, "What is your question?"

"I…I didn't know I had to have a question. What kind of question?"

Liam bends toward me. "The question you want to ask the cards. It can be anything. Didn't you say you wanted a partner?"

I look at Liam, then at Constance. I'm starting to sweat.

"I want to know if things will stop being complicated."

"Complicated with someone?"

"Mm-hm."

Constance nods again. Then, as smoothly as she can, she places the cards in line on the satin cloth and takes a deep breath. Her fingertips dance on the cards, stop, move again, then she takes one card out, which she places to my right without flipping it, then another one to my left, and another one between both of them. That's three cards in front of me, face down.

"This specific tarot spread asks for guidance to find what needs to be done to overcome anything that's standing between you"—she shows the card to my right—"and another person"—she shows the one to my left. "This card, here, in the middle, is the challenge, what stands between you two."

She goes back to the deck and takes out a fourth card, which she places right in front of me, in a horizontal position.

"This is the solution. It's in this position because it can't be good or bad. It just *is*. Shall we start? I'm going to flip over the first card, the one that will tell us where you are."

She proceeds. The card shows a character on a cloud surrounded by a multitude of golden cups.

"Seven of Cups. That card is upright. It tells us you have many options, many good options. You're struggling to make a choice because they all seem promising."

I swallow and try to keep a poker face. This sounds very familiar. But they probably all do. She reaches to the card number two, to my left, and flips it as well. It shows another character carrying a bunch of sticks on their back.

"The Ten of Wands. Another Upright card. It means the person you're thinking of is burdened with too many responsibilities. The Ten symbolizes the end of a cycle, with which comes great rewards and fulfillment, but also great exhaustion."

Constance lifts her head to look at me. She must notice I'm not breathing because she says, "Is that possible?"

I nod silently. I'm thinking of Stephie who just broke up with Frank, of course. It's scary how spot-on it is. She goes on with the card in the middle. It shows the same character twice, carving two round symbols on the ground, while a bunch of other similar symbols are already finished around them.

"Upright Eight of Pentacles. The card of apprenticeship. You're learning a skill, Alex, and you're dedicated to doing it right. It means your perseverance will create something beautiful. In the meantime, it's normal to make mistakes."

"That's the challenge?"

"That's what stands between you two, yes. This is all mostly positive. All upright cards. Things are looking bright so far. There's only one card left, which will tell us about what needs to be done to overcome the situation."

She reaches for the last card, the one that's in a horizontal position. She flips it to reveal…instructions on how to use the deck. Black on white. I can see in her face how completely destabilized she is.

"This is…this is highly unusual, as you can guess."

She strokes her chin, then her cheek.

"I guess I forgot to remove it when I got the deck. I told you it was a new one."

"What does it mean?"

She laughs and picks up the card to discard it besides her.

"It doesn't mean anything. That card wasn't supposed to be there. I'll pick a new one. Let's see…."

She takes a moment to gather her forces and runs her fingers over the cards that are still lined in front of her, on the satin cloth. Her hand suddenly gets dragged down like a magnet on one of the cards, which she places where the previous one was.

She takes a deep breath and flips it….

…To reveal another blank card. A list of rules.

Now her eyes are wider than ever. She is speechless. Liam looks at the desk in complete disbelief. "How is that even possible?"

Constance replies, "One of them, sure. It's a mistake. It doesn't belong in the deck. We take it out. But twice? I think the cards are trying to tell us something."

This is so awkward. I want to leave, or at least to end this tarot session. I need to pee. Constance takes the blank card between her fingers and moves it aside where she put the other one.

"So, this has happened. I think we need to see what else the deck has to tell us. Shall I pick another card?"

I shrug. I'm not sure what I can say at this point.

The new card she picks actually belongs in the deck. It has a character with a crown on it, holding a blossoming stick, and sitting on a throne decorated with a lion and a lizard biting its own tail. Constance calms down and says, "King of Wands. It symbolizes burning energy. Infinite possibilities. Clarity after chaos. Contemplation."

CHAPTER 11

I PROBABLY LOOK shaken when we leave Constance's house, because on the way back, Liam keeps telling me about every way tarot is fake. "You see, the cards don't *know* stuff. You do. You're the one that puts meaning in them. They are keys that open doors, but only you can tell what you see inside. And only you can decide what to make of it."

"I know. But it was so spot on, it was scary."

"Who were you thinking of?"

"Not telling."

"Was it me?"

I turn my head toward him and smirk. "Do you want it to be you?"

"I don't know! It sounds risky with the solution the cards gave us. What if we get thrown into another dimension or something like that if we kiss?"

"I get thrown in another dimension every time I see your eyes, bro."

"Aww! That's so gay."

"Thanks, you too."

"Hashtag yes-homo."

We take the same road on the way back as we did to get there, since it was so nice with the park and the river. We stop talking about the tarot reading for a bit, until we take a break for stretches and water. Liam looks at me with the straightest face he can pull off. "It was Jayden, right?"

I admire his perspicacity for a short moment and roll my eyes. He goes on, "It can't be Gabriel. You're not invested in him enough for that. And it's not at the point where it's 'complicated' with him…."

"It's not complicated with Jayden either."

"So, it's not him…. Oh, wait. Is it…?"

He pauses to observe my face, suddenly realizing what he's getting at.

"It's Stephie, isn't it?"

I nod. I'm a bit ashamed of myself.

"Yeah, it makes sense. And you said the reading was spot on?"

"All of it. How I have too many choices, how she's busy with responsibilities and caring for herself, how I suck at everything…."

"What? The cards never said that 'you suck at everything.' You invented that."

"The card of apprenticeship, the obstacle between me

and Stephie. Your aunt said it meant that I was still learning and making mistakes. It's like, the polite tarot way of saying I suck."

"No, it's not. You're distorting the meaning so you can blame yourself for something that's not your fault. Don't do that."

"Let's go before it's dark."

We ride in silence for a good stretch of time. Liam can't stand when people put themselves down. I remember, once, Stephie said she thought she was ugly in front of him, and he couldn't believe his ears, which is understandable because Stephie is definitely the cutest girl at school. He spent days just telling her every way she's beautiful, he's good at that. The only person who has the right to put themself down is himself.

We eventually arrive at his house. We are about to part ways when he says, "You know, with Stephie…you shouldn't worry about it. I'm sure it will all work out."

"Yeah. Thanks."

"Also, you don't suck. Byyye! See you Monday!"

I wave at him and cycle uphill back home. My brother is playing videogames with João in the living room, while I find my dad in the kitchen, busy baking muffins. I scavenge for utensils and bowls to lick. My dad asks me how the ride was, and I say, with a spatula in my mouth, "Short, but nice. We went to see Liam's aunt in Repentigny. She's pretty cool, she lives in an old stone house with a gay friend of hers. She gave me a tarot reading!"

"Hahaha! How was it?"

"It was interesting. I liked it. Very insightful."

"I've never done that. I don't even know what it looks like."

"You play cards and you chat about your life."

"Did you tell her your father is a fantastic cook?"

I nod without conviction, my head inside a big aluminum bowl. There's a spot at the bottom with tons of batter, but my tongue just can't reach it. My phone buzzes twice from the pocket in the back of my cycling vest. I pull my face out of the bowl. Both messages are from Stephie. The first one is just an email address, and the other one says,

This is the journalist's contact, for your brother!

I tell my dad. "Did Virgil tell you about his plan to tell the papers about his drag show? I have the email for the journalist at the *Metro* newspaper. You should probably handle that."

"I think he mentioned it in the car yesterday, between two excited hiccups. Send it to me, I'll forward it to his troop leader."

I copy Stephie's message and send it to my dad, then I go back to Stephie's message and write:

Thank you, you're the best xx

To which she replies with a GIF of a little girl looking sassy and throwing her hair behind her shoulders. I go to my bedroom for some privacy, and I send her pictures I took during the day: one of the parks by the river, another from when we crossed that long bridge between Montréal and the North Shore, and a selfie we took with Constance before leaving.

It looks like you had a nice day! Who's that?

I tell her about Liam's aunt and the purpose of our trip. And the tarot reading.

There was a mix-up with her cards. She left the cards with the instructions and the rules in the deck and pulled both of them.

Oh no! Was the reading good, though?

Liam's aunt said yes, but it was a bit complicated. I didn't understand most of what she said.

I try to find good half-truths without telling her the crucial parts. I change the subject.

What about you? Having fun with your grandma?

She sends me a picture of Micheline, her grandmother, working on a cross-stitch piece on her veranda. Then she sends another one, of Stephie's knees and the embroidery project she is working on. In the middle of the hoop, it reads "Boys are trash" in fancy letters, and she's cross-stitching flowers all around it.

So pretty!!

My grandma didn't say anything when she saw it, just smiled. I think she likes it.

It's beautiful. Did you tell her I say hi?

Just did. She says hi too and wants to know how you are.

I'm very good, Micheline, thank you! I'm a bit tired from cycling all day, but nothing a bit of rest won't fix. May I ask you the same? It seems like you're having nice weather in the Eastern townships, from what I can tell from the pictures Stephie sent me!

This is going too far; I'll just tell her you're doing good.

Boooo!

★ ★ ★

On Monday at school, I hear the new rumor even before getting to my locker: apparently, Raquel is taking a break and will be homeschooled for a little while. Stephie is so upset that I can almost see steam coming out of her ears. She says, "It has to be because of what happened Friday with Sullivan. She's being humiliated and bullied because of what Viktor did. It's the most unfair thing I've ever heard of."

"It makes me throw up in my mouth a little."

"I don't ever want anything to do with a boy ever again."

I can't help but smile. First, because that would give me more chances with her, and second, because I don't believe her at all; she's too much of a flirt to keep such ambitious promises.

"Don't look at me like that! It's true. They just mess up every time they have a chance to be responsible, and they expect everyone around them to clean up after them. I'm so done."

"So, I guess you're gonna keep cross-stitching these 'boys are trash' embroideries, then?"

"You bet. They're so relaxing to make. If you can't find a reason to carry on, do it to spite them. Do you want one?"

"Maybe not 'boys are trash.' My brother would be offended. Maybe more something along the lines of 'boys are gross?' 'Boys are smelly?'"

"I'll consider those."

I have lunch with the cheerleading squad. When I sit between Jayden and Caroline, everyone's discussing the rumors about Raquel, but with less anger than Stephie. Cynthia says, "I just hope things will be less tense, now. You should have been there this morning in my French class. People were at each other's throats."

The subject rapidly shifts to tonight's basketball match, where they are going to show their entirely new cheer routine for the first time. Jayden tries to explain it to me while Cynthia and Caroline mimic the movements with their fingers on the table, but it's kind of hard to follow, especially as Jayden constantly adds details about musical cues.

"So, let's say we're at the intermission. They're probably going to play ten seconds of 'We Will Rock You' or something dull like that. *Boom-boom, tsh, boom-boom, tsh.* The players leave the floor, and our music starts. *Bam bam bam! Too-doo-doo-doo-doo.* The announcer says our name: the Wolverines' cheer team! *Boom-tsh, boom-tsh, boom-tsh.* We arrive in formation. Five, six, seven, eight. We get in pairs. I'm with Caroline on that one. I hold her by the waist. Cathy gets on Dominic's shoulders. Just you wait till you see it, they've been practicing all summer. Then the music goes *shakashakashak!* And while the paired teams do a balance movement, Cathy jumps in the air and does a freaking backflip if I've ever seen one. Mind blown. We rejoice in a circle, then make two lines. Jump, jump, jump. The music goes *na na na na na na.* Cynthia, Mi-Linh, and Laetitia, that girl over there, they start doing cartwheels between the lines. The music slows down, *dun dun dun,* but it's not over. We spread out all around the floor. And when the music goes *fadala dala,* we have this special move—"

I start laughing and stop him with my hands. "Stop! It looks—and sounds—amazing, but I want to keep some surprises for when I see it."

"So, you're coming? Nice!"

"Of course. You invited me."

"Yeah, I did, but you never know. It's going to be great. I mean, not the basketball game, but…. I mean unless you're into basketball."

Cynthia asks me, "Is our team any good, this year? We're so busy practicing and performing, we don't even think about it."

I don't say anything because Caroline replies, "Pay attention! They haven't lost a single game yet."

"The school year just started. They played, what—two times?"

"Three! Oh my God, Cyn. It's late October. School hasn't 'just started.'"

Caroline has a way of saying "oh my God" with her European accent that always makes me smile. Jayden turns toward me. "Who are you going with?"

"Who am I going with where?"

"To the game. You're not bringing anyone?"

"I had no clue I needed to."

"You should. Especially if you're not into basketball. It might get boring between our glorious appearances."

I think for a moment. Who could I invite to see Jayden cheer? Liam has a swimming practice, and I don't want Stephie to know about my crush on Jayden. It would be weird to invite her to a basketball game. She knows I hate watching sports. But she also knows I'm becoming friends with the cheerleading squad, so I guess I could play that card....

"I think I'll be fine. I'll do homework between each of your 'glorious appearances.'"

Caroline goes "aww" as Cynthia tells Jayden, "See the length he goes to to come and watch us? That's dedication."

Without giving me any time to process what his friend just said, Jayden looks cross and replies, "It's they."

146

"They?"

"Alex uses they. The length *they* go to. We've been over this."

Cynthia apologizes to me, which I appreciate, but I don't think much about the mistake. I'm just seduced by how caring Jayden can be, behind his judgmental manner. That's when I decide that I could live in a world where he's my boyfriend.

Caroline, probably feeling awkward, changes the subject. "It's Halloween in two days. What are you all doing?"

Cynthia says, "Trick-or-treating with my two sisters. I'll probably go to Cathy's Halloween party on Friday, though."

Cathy is the captain of the cheerleading squad. She's not the oldest, but she definitely looks the fittest. She's very popular. Caroline replies, "My parents would never let me go." She whispers to me, "There's going to be alcohol."

Jayden says, "Alex and I are going to the LGBT+ Center's Halloween party."

"That sounds cool! Will you wear costumes?"

Jayden looks at me. "I don't know. Will we?"

"I think it's strongly suggested but not mandatory."

"I'm not that much into costumes, to be honest."

"You should put on your old gymnastic onesie. People will love it."

"I said it was stretchy, but not *that* stretchy!"

We both laugh while Caroline and Cynthia try to figure out what's so funny. The bell rings and we pack our stuff.

In math and English, I can't concentrate on anything. I keep replaying the scene at the lunch table when Jayden corrected Cynthia about the pronouns I use. Maybe Cynthia and Caroline are right. Maybe Jaydex is meant to be a thing.

When school is over, I walk slowly down the halls, letting people pass me on the staircase. I move like a sloth. There're forty-five minutes before the basketball game, and I don't have much to do beside homework, so I try to stretch the time. I guess I could finally get started on my book report, which is due next week, but that sounds boring. So boring it makes me nervous.

Stephie is still packing her school bag when I arrive at the lockers. She has her new fall jacket on that she bought with her mom two weeks ago. It's made of taupe felt. She had already taken it off when I arrived this morning, but now I can see how it fits her. It goes way down below her waist and covers most of her peach skirt, with only an inch or so showing. It's something a stylish French woman would wear in a movie. Or maybe one of those girls from the Japanese cartoons Liam is obsessed with. She notices me. "Hey, sweetie! You're still here?"

"Yeah, I'm taking it slow. Saving my energy to create the ultimate book report."

It stings every time I lie to her, even if it's a half-truth. She says, "I love your enthusiasm. How was your day?"

"Normal. Yours?"

"Okay, I guess. I finally talked to Frank in my English class."

My heart starts pounding. It's all my fault. She would still be upset with him if it wasn't for what I told her. I already have regrets.

"How did it go?"

She sighs very loudly. "He knows he messed up. He wants to make up for it. Blah blah blah."

"Do you think he's sincere?"

"I don't know. I'll see. I told him I was sorry for how harshly I reacted. He said I didn't need to be. It was kind of nice, you know?"

"Yeah."

"Anyway. I said I'd unblock his number on my phone. To be continued, I guess. But hey, I gotta catch the bus. You're staying late, or what?"

"I was thinking of going to the library to get some work done."

"Wow! I'm impressed. That's unlike you."

We smile at each other. She puts her backpack on and points a finger gun at me. "Bam! I'll see you on Insta."

"Uggh! I'm dead."

★ ★ ★

I start my book report using one of the library computers, but everything I write feels like nonsense. I don't care. It doesn't count for much in the semester. It's silly that we have to do so much work just to add little decimals to our report cards here and there.

I think it's the first time I've stayed late at the school library. The atmosphere is peaceful without the background noise from the classrooms and school halls. There's a chess club meeting, but they don't make a sound except for sweat drops hitting the tables. Earlier, a mom came to talk to the librarian about her son's fines for not returning books over the summer. It was all very silly and dramatic—she made quite a scene. The guy owed something like two hundred dollars. Both adults were whispering, but you could tell it was heated.

At ten to four, I save my work on my hamburger-shaped USB stick and go down to the gym, where loud rock music is already playing. A lot of people are waiting to watch the game. Mostly parents and siblings of the basketball players, I guess. I don't think I know anyone on the team. I try to see if Jayden's parents might be there. I only said hi quickly the other day, when I visited his house, but I think I could recognize them. I browse through the faces, but I don't see any that look familiar. It makes me a bit sad that Jayden's parents would miss their kid's performance, considering how excited he was about it. Maybe they're used to him shining in front of an audience by now, and there's nothing special to it anymore. Still, it makes me sad.

Retractable bleachers have been pulled out from the wall, giving a completely different feel to the gym. It's the first sports thing I've been to. The score board, usually shut down during the day, is all illuminated and reads *Home* and *Visitor*. These novelties almost make me excited for the game.

Cheers ring out as a first batch of players come out of the changing rooms. From what I can gather, the orange team is from Simonne Monet-Chartrand and the black one is from Pauline-Julien, a school in the north of the city. Parents yell names, hoping their child will wave at them, but it's useless, the sound is lost in the terrible acoustics of the gym, and the guys probably don't care. They sit on the benches on both sides of the floor, and coaches give each team instructions.

I play on my phone until the rock music fades out. People start clapping, and as the basketball players stretch in preparation for the game, the cheerleading squad arrives from a corner where they were getting ready. A bunch of them are holding giant, decorated foam letters spelling out the name of the team (W-O-L-V-E-R-I-N-E-S-!) while others are *pompoming* up and down between the letters. Jayden is holding the O and doing a great job, I'm sure. They're all wearing orange and white shiny suits and fancy hairdos with huge bows and ribbons, except Jayden, of course, who has short hair and is wearing a bandana. It looks badass. I take a picture of him holding his big O, to show him later what a cute dork he is, but as the squad leaves the floor, I peek at the picture and decide to keep it to myself: his expression is angelic. He is smiling so big, and the fluorescent lights on the ceiling make his eyes all sparkly. If he sees it, he'll probably hate it and ask me to delete it from my phone because it's not taken from a weird angle like every other picture on his Instagram account.

A whistle blows, and the game is on. The players run after the ball like a flock of kittens. I watch for a moment, before getting seriously bored. I can't let it show too much, though, since I'm surrounded by active supporters: they shout, yell, sing. I'm already overwhelmed by the noise. Jayden was right. I should have brought someone with me.

After what seems like forever, all the players leave the floor to hydrate themselves and lie on the benches. The ball has bounced and passed through the baskets to the joy and satisfaction of the crowd. "We Will Rock You" is now playing. Who will rock who? Don't know, don't care. But I start paying attention as the announcer's voice proclaims, "Please welcome back the Wolverines Cheer Squad!"

The music fades to some fat techno beats, and the squad's members run out to cover the floor. Now, besides that there's an epic backflip at some point, I don't remember a single thing Jayden told me about this new routine, and all I can think of is his beatboxing rendition of the music cues (*boom-tsh, boom-tsh*), but it's still very exciting for me to see it in action. Their first appearance at the beginning of the game was silly compared to this. They are coordinated and synchronized. They twirl, throw each other in every direction, jump, and dance. It's much more physical than I expected—it's impressive. Suddenly, there it goes: one of them ejects herself from another cheerleader's shoulders and does a backflip that makes the audience gasp, clap, and go wild. It really was mind blowing.

The show goes on for a couple more minutes, and pairs of cheerleaders hold a teammate in the air. I had no clue Jayden had that kind of strength. I wonder if he could lift me up like that by himself.

Before they're done, my phone vibrates on my lap. I have a message.

It's from Gabriel.

Hey, Alex! How are you?

I swallow. Not now. I type quickly.

Good, you?

I'm fine. I was wondering if you wanted to hang out?

I look at the screen, then at Jayden, who's killing it with some last dance moves. The music suggests the show is about to end. The announcer says, "Please give a round of applause to the Wolverines Cheer Squad!"

The crowd starts making a lot of noise. I turn my phone off, get up, and leave as the cheerleaders exit.

CHAPTER 12

I TOLD GABRIEL I didn't have any time to see him tonight. It's partly true: I need to get ready for the Halloween party at the LGBT+ Center in a couple of days. But the truth is, he's not on my priority list. He tried to make some small talk, but I kept all my answers short and vague. I didn't even use a single emoji. Maybe I'm being mean. It's not like he doesn't deserve it. He has some humble pie to swallow before I can trust him.

When I get home, Virgil is at his usual spot at the computer. As I close the door, he turns around and removes his headphones. "Dad spoke to the journalist. We're meeting her tomorrow."

"Sweet! Are you excited?"

"Yes, very. Do you want to be there?"

"Why would I?"

"I don't know. Dad said the journalist remembered you and wanted a quote from you or something."

"Sure. Anything for the best brother I could have dreamed of."

"Awww!"

"That doesn't include your smelliness. You can't actually smell things in dreams."

"And that's a fact! Can't disagree."

After dinner, I have a slow evening. From my bed, I text Jayden to congratulate him, and he's all like:

I messed up so many times! I missed tons of cues, and I forgot moves.

Really? I assure you none of that was obvious. And I was watching you.

You're weird. But everyone on the squad noticed. They'll probably make fun of me at the next practice.

I decide to send him the beautiful picture I took of him holding that big, foam O at the beginning. If I wait until tomorrow at school before showing him, he'll want me to delete it and it would be hard to say no, but if I don't tell him and he finds out about it later, it would be really weird, and he'll think I'm obsessed or something.

Eww, I look like a blob on this.

A blob? No you don't. I like that picture.

Don't you dare post this anywhere.

*Now, I won't even need your gymnastics videos to
blackmail you!*

Ugh.

I think it's sad that Jayden is ashamed of the way he
looks, but I always hate my face in pictures, too. Maybe it's
because I'm always just mimicking facial expressions I know I
should make without really understanding why, and it creates
a distance between what I wish my face was saying and what
it actually looks like. Humans are weird and do weird things.

I message Stephie to tell her about my brother going to
talk to the journalist. She replies:

That's awesome! Good for him.

*My dad told me we're supposed to meet at a coffee
shop near the subway entrance, along with Virgil's
scout leader.*

You're going too?

Yeah, Virgil wanted me to come.

He loves you so much. He's such a sweetheart.

*I'll let you have him if you want. What are you doing,
tonight?*

Just watching a terrible movie with my dad and chatting with people online. You?

I am itching to ask her if that includes Frank. But I must be better than that. It's none of my business. I should focus on us, on what we are, Stephie and me, rather than Frank and her. Frank isn't a threat to me. I take a deep breath and send her,

Same, without the terrible movie. But I'd rather be cuddling with you right now, lol.

Which I instantly regret. Who writes "lol" nowadays? Me, apparently. She replies instantly.

That would be nice. It's getting kinda late, though.

Tomorrow you could come over, once we're done with the interview.

No can do, I'm babysitting after 6. Wednesday?

It's the LGBT Youth Center's Halloween party.

Oh right, it's this Wednesday. Samira told me she heard that you were going on a date with Jayden?

I'm petrified. Since when does Stephie know? I'm probably blushing because my face starts warming uncontrollably. I don't know what to tell her, but at the same time, I guess it would make sense to her that I have a crush on Jayden, since I stopped having lunch at her table to be with the cheerleading squad. I bet it was Cynthia who told Samira who told Stephie. No one can keep a secret in this school.

Should I just go ahead and tell her? While I'm debating internally, she says,

You two would be so cute together.

Why does everyone say that? I don't want Stephie to think I'd make a cute couple with Jayden; I want her to think I'd make a cute couple with her. I'm sabotaging this whole thing myself. I'm regret everything. And why is she bringing that up now when we were making cuddling plans? I finally reply,

It's not really a date, I just wanted to show him the Youth group. Also, he keeps saying I'm not his type.

That's too bad. Do you like him?

You know me. I like everyone!

Ha ha! True. A real crowd pleaser.

Anyway, do you want to come to the party?

The only reason I ask her is that I know she'll say no—we went to the Youth Group meetings together a couple of times and she didn't really like it.

Nah, I'm good. One party a week is enough, and I think Leah is planning a game night at her house on Thursday.

And no one invited me?

Do you want to come? We only discussed it at lunch today, and you weren't there.

I'll think about it. It would be nice. When was the last time we did something with everyone together?

Probably that sleepover we had at the beginning of school at Samira's place.

Right, that was a disaster.

Stop it, it was hilarious.

With the flood in the basement and the fire Samira's mom started in the kitchen?

You had tons of fun, admit it.

It doesn't change that it was a disaster.

Fine. But this time, it's at Leah's house. Her mom is amazing, you'll see.

I'll consider it. Hey, I didn't tell you who messaged me during the basketball game!

You went to a basketball game?! You've changed, Ciel Sousa.

Ugh. I really messed up. That should teach me not to lie to Stephie. I'm not a good enough liar to keep it up. I decide to unveil it all.

Yeah, the cheerleading squad wanted me to come see their new routine.

So you didn't even stay after school to work on your book report like you told me you were? How many things are you hiding from me? Next thing I'll learn, you're a Russian spy and you have a husband and four kids in Novgorod!

Hey, I did work on my book report, for real! And my Russian husband is a good man for me, don't judge our union.

Alright, sorry. So, who messaged you? Certainly not your Russian husband, you're undercover.

Gabriel. He wanted to hang out.

I would have preferred it if you told me it was your Russian husband.

★ ★ ★

During French class, while Liam was telling me anecdotes about his aunt Constance (including everything he knew about that curse she put on his dad, I can't get enough details about that), Stephie stopped by our table to say hi.

"I have a telegram for Mx. Ciel Sousa."

She takes an envelope out of her pink portfolio and gracefully puts it on my desk before prancing away to the back of the class. Liam snorts. "You two are delight to watch, you know that?"

"It's not an actual telegram."

The envelope isn't made of regular paper. It has texture to it, like it's been handmade from recycled materials. It's an antique ivory color and smells like peach. I recognize the fancy perfume she got last Christmas from her dad. On the back, my name is written in Stephie's nicest handwriting. Liam whispers, "Open it."

"I'm savoring the moment, don't rush me."

"The class is about to start."

I turn toward the back of the class, where Stephie is sitting with Leah. She looks a bit nervous. I take off the unicorn sticker holding the envelope closed and pull the letter out, to Liam's satisfaction. Around the message, there's a frame made from ivy and roses. I'll have to ask Stephie where she gets her stationery.

My gayest one,

Destiny has us jumping through hoops like felines in a circus. Time is healing and the kingdoms shall rejoice. But until then, it's totally fine if you want to do stuff by yourself. We're not tied by any contract. Don't be ashamed of looking somewhere else. You don't have to lie to me, I'm your best friend.

I'll get it.
Tell your Russian husband I say hi,
Stephanie

Liam tries to peek at the letter while I'm reading, but only catches a glimpse of it before I flip it.

"'Your Russian husband?' Did I miss something?"

"Yeah, just one of the many things I've been hiding from people."

"It's okay. You're allowed to have your secret garden. Are you changing your name to his?"

"Nah. We're a modern couple."

Ms. Campeau closes the classroom door, indicating the beginning of class. After reminding us that there's only one week left to give her our book reports, she starts the lesson, and I put Stephie's letter safely in my bag. I'm touched she went to the trouble of writing it. She seemed fine yesterday when we were chatting, but maybe she was hurt to learn I've been lying to her. The letter's tone is bittersweet. I feel guilty.

When class is over, Liam and I wait for Stephie, and we end up walking to the lockers with Leah too. I wish I had some time alone with Stephie to talk to her about the whole thing, but it'll have to wait. Leah formally invites us to her modest Halloween party. "It's going to be great. My mom is getting us pizza. We have a futon and an extra mattress that we can put on the floor, plus my bed, so we can all sleep there. If you want to, of course. And you're invited too, Liam!"

"That's so sweet of you, Leah. But I don't really know anyone who's going to be there, besides Ciel."

"There will be me, Stephie, Samira, Océane, Ciel, and maybe you. That's all."

"I'll think about it. Thanks for the invitation!"

"No problem."

At lunch, I tell Caroline, Cynthia, and Jayden how much I liked their new routine from the basketball game. They make a big deal of all the mistakes Jayden did, and he starts listing all the moments the two others messed up. It's really hard to convince them none of it was noticeable.

"Didn't you leave before the end of the game, though? During our last appearance, we literally fell on the floor like dominos."

"Because of you, Jayden!"

"I know! I'm sorry!"

"People even said we brought bad luck to the team."

"Why? Did we lose?"

"Well, duh! You were there."

"I wasn't really paying attention."

"Then don't try to tell us our mistakes didn't show."

"I was there to see you, not a bunch of dudes chasing a ball."

"That's valid. I don't even know the rules for basketball."

"There's a ball. A basket. Two teams. The team who puts the ball in the basket the most wins. It's super easy, Cyn."

"Well, the difference between you and me, Caro, is that I don't really care."

★ ★ ★

As we planned, when I get home from school, Virgil, my dad, and I take the bus to the subway station to meet the *Metro* journalist at a coffee shop nearby. Virgil is going to the interview in full drag, wearing our pink curly wig and a golden evening dress covered in sequins. Over his tights, he put on his pink legwarmers that match the wig. Needless to say, the people on the bus have a lot of feelings about his outfit, especially the older teenagers who got on at the private college on Rosemont Boulevard, who came to ask for selfies with him.

"Don't forget to tag me, @DoloresvonTragic, if you post them on Instagram!"

One of the teenagers replies, "Keep slaying, sis!"

Virgil's scout leader, Bagheera, is already at the coffee shop when we arrive. It's the first time I have actually met him, although I've seen him here and there whenever I've accompanied my dad to Virgil's scout events. He is tall and very muscular, with black hair all over his body like a stereotypical lumberjack. Or a black panther, like the *Jungle Book* character he's named after. But that's where the comparison ends: when he sees us, a big smile appears on his face, and he suddenly fills the place with more warmth than the espresso machine with its milk steamer could ever do.

"Virgil! Lucas! And you must be Virgil's sibling? He told us all about you! What's your name?"

I blush, partly because my brother has been talking about me enough for his scout leader to remember who I am, and partly because such an attractive man is interested in me.

"Alex. You can call me Ciel."

"Ciel is a beautiful nickname."

I smile and get all giddy. As I sit down at the table Bagheera was waiting at with a coffee, my dad takes our orders (two white hot chocolates) and goes to the counter to get them.

"Bagheera is a nickname as well. We all have to use *Jungle Book*-related names as scout leaders."

Virgil gets very excited. "Oh! Oh! Will I get to know your real name?!"

"Haha! I'm not sure I can trust you with that. It's a national secret."

Virgil keeps pleading his cause when a woman with a trench coat enters the coffee shop. She looks familiar. Virgil's outfit catches her eye, and she sees me, and comes to our table.

"Alex! How have you been since the last time I saw you?"

I recognize Melinda, the *Metro* journalist. "Good, and you?"

"Very good, very good."

She shakes my hand vigorously and turns toward Bagheera. "You must be Lucas?"

We all laugh, except Virgil, who gasps and asks Bagheera, "Wait, is that your real name? You have the same name as our dad?"

The journalist apologizes. "Oh, sorry, I thought that was you. Bagheera, then?"

Bagheera shakes her hand as well. My dad arrives from behind Melinda with three cups and introduces himself. The journalist goes to order something for herself, but in the meantime, a group of people got in and take forever to place their order, leaving us in an awkward silence while we sip our hot chocolates. She finally comes back and puts her recorder on the table.

"Alright, thank you for taking the time to meet me. When I read your email, Lucas, I was just fascinated by how beautiful and amusing this story is. I'm sure it's going to be a lot of fun to cover. And can I just say, Virgil, how amazing your outfit is? Our photographer is supposed to join us in half an hour or so. Would you mind us taking some pictures?"

"Whoa, cool! No, it's fine."

As if she had to ask twice!

"Perfect. So first, I'll ask you, Bagheera, to explain to me what's happening. It's the district's cub scout troop, am I right?"

"Precisely. As we do every year, we're organizing a fund-raiser for our scout retreat, which will be in Rawdon this winter. I asked our cubs to come up with themes, and Virgil here had the idea for a drag talent show."

"Awesome. What inspired you, Virgil?"

"Oh, I'm a drag queen myself. I love drag. I love putting on shows. I like the dancing and the costumes."

"And you wanted to share this passion with the others in your troop?"

"Yeah, I guess."

"That's great. What do you like about drag?"

Virgil giggles and looks around, as if to make sure no one else can hear him, before telling Melinda, "I like seeing other people's reactions. It makes them think. They see boys and girls as different species, like cats and dogs, like we're opposites, but it's not true. There are boys who enjoy girl things, girls who enjoy boy things. Wait, girl things and boy things don't even exist. I mean, I think people should be allowed to be who they are, and there's much more than just 'boys' and 'girls.' Everyone would be a lot less stressed and angry all the time if they could just explore different ways of being themselves."

Melinda's eyes go wide and she turns toward my father in surprise. Dad just smiles and taps Virgil's back lovingly. Melinda says, "Wow, that's…that's very well said. Thank you."

"You're welcome."

"Is there anyone you look up to, who inspires you? A celebrity crush?"

"Alex, my sibling. They're out at school and they get bullied a lot for it, but I'm sure a lot of people see them around and it makes them feel better, because then they know they're not alone."

"You two get along well?"

"We fight sometimes, but I guess that's normal."

I never thought I could feel so much love for my brother. It's like I'm seeing him for the first time. I say, "Virgil teaches me a lot, too. I'm happy he can be that confident in his self-expression. I always feel like I have to protect myself from the world, that I don't deserve to be seen for who I am. He reminds me how important it is."

Virgil listens to me with his eyes sparkling. I feel the urge to add, "Now if he could only smell a bit less, that would great."

CHAPTER 13

THE FIRST TIME, it feels like a bee bumping into my head when I'm cycling, only I'm in Science and Technology class, and I'm sitting at my desk beside Jayden. I turn around to where the projectile came from, but I don't see anything suspicious. I can't find anything on the floor either. It must have been my imagination.

The second time, the thing that hit the top of my head bounces on my desk. It's a piece of eraser. It looks like it was cut with a pair of scissors. Wasting perfectly good eraser like that. My heart bleeds. I look behind me again, knowing very well where it must have come from. One of the cool guys in the back. Gabriel is staring at me, because of course he is, but it couldn't possibly be him, unless he thinks that's the new cool and hip way to flirt with someone. Sullivan, perhaps? The thing is, he looks busy with the worksheet Mr. Brazeau handed out a moment ago. It must be one of the other two, they look distracted. I get back to work.

Then, the third time, I can't handle it anymore. I take my phone out of my pocket. Making sure the teacher doesn't see me, I text Gabriel.

Hey, can you tell whoever is throwing eraser bits at me to stop?

I send the message and wait. Two more pieces of rubber hit me before my phone shows the Read check mark. And that's only the pieces that got to me. I'm sure a lot of them missed or hit other people by mistake.

I told him, sorry about that.

No worries, thanks.

The attack stops. I'm telling myself that Gabriel isn't that bad after all, and that it's a good idea to have an ally on the dark side, when yet another piece of eraser hits my head, falls through my collar, and down the back of my dress. The object slides along my skin and I curse this life.

Jayden notices how agitated I am and whispers, "Can't find the answer?"

"Someone is throwing eraser pieces at me."

"What, really? That must be what hit me earlier."

"I'm the target. I've even got one inside my dress."

"Ugh. What an ass."

I text Gabriel again. He can't be that useless.

He's at it again.

I know, sorry. I told him. He won't listen.

I sigh heavily and put my phone away. I count the minutes before the class ends. The eraser-pieces throwing eventually stops, probably because the assailant used up all of his resources.

The bell finally rings, and I hurry up to the French classroom before anyone like Gabriel or Frank can come talk to me. Liam is already there, apparently waiting for me because when I get through the door, he throws a newspaper in my hands.

"Here's your copy, 'inspirational sibling!' Page nine."

I flip through the *Metro* to find a big picture of my brother with his pink wig, giving attitude. The picture was taken from above his head—the photographer was quite tall—and the background is blurred. Liam reads from his own copy: "When asked who inspires him, the ten-year-old unequivocally answers: 'My sibling, Alex. They are transgender and open about it at their school, even though it gets them bullied. I'm sure it makes a lot of people feel better, because then, they know they're not alone.' That's the sweetest thing ever!"

"That's not exactly what he said. The words were changed."

"Yeah, journalists do that sometimes. You also get quoted, at the end!"

"'Virgil teaches me a lot, too. I'm happy he can be that

171

confident in his self-expression. I always feel like I have to protect myself against the world, that I don't deserve to be seen for who I am. He reminds me how important it is.'"

"Is that what you said?"

"Meh. Something like that, I guess, but less cheesy."

"Yeah, it's unlike you not to mention your brother's smell. But it's a really good article!"

"He's going to be ecstatic about it. We probably won't hear the end of it for the next twelve months."

I stop Stephie when she enters the classroom to show her the newspaper. She laughs when she sees the picture.

"This is amazing. Look at his face! It's like he's about to jump at your throat or bite off your nose like a chihuahua. I hope your dad frames it and puts it on a wall so I can see it every time I visit."

Stephie gives me back the paper and goes to her usual seat. At the end of class, I ask Liam if he's still planning to come to the LGBT+ Center tonight for the Halloween party.

"Of course! Just don't expect me to wear a costume. I'm coming straight from practice."

"They'll be doing spooky makeup in the evening."

"Cool, then I'll be a moth. I relate to moths on a spiritual level."

"I could be a lamp. I'll bring a shade from home and just wear it like a hat. With my silky bathrobe. A sexy lamp! You'll be my moth, and I'll be your lamp!"

"Really, you'd be my lamp? You're going to make me cry. That's beautiful."

★ ★ ★

My dad had already picked up a copy of today's *Metro* at work, so I get to keep the one Liam gave me. As I expected, Virgil is jumping all around.

"I can't wait for the show! It's going to be so great. There will be loootsss of people. We'll have the best winter camp ever!"

I check Dolores von Tragic's Instagram with him. It got several dozen new followers today, since the article mentioned the account.

"Woooh! I'm famous. What am I going to wear for the show? Dad! I need a new dress!"

My dad tries to calm him down. "You already have enough. Maybe after Halloween, the stores will have discounts on costumes. We can go check, but I'm sure you have something that could do."

My brother sighs. As I pack my bag to go to the LGBT+ Center, I say, "You know what? I think I know someone who could lend you something fabulous. It's not a dress, but you would look amazing in it."

"What is it?"

"I'll ask him if it's okay first because I don't want to get your hopes too high. But I can tell you it's very sparkly."

My dad asks me, "Wait, where do you think you're going with that lamp shade?"

"It's for my costume. We're having Halloween tonight, at the LGBT+ Center."

"You're going to be a lamp?"

"Yup, exactly. And Liam is my moth."

"Sure. I won't ask any more questions."

"Believe me, Dad, it's better that way."

I leave for the Village, taking the familiar route from the bus stop to the orange line to Beaudry station. It's way too cold to cycle all the way there, and anyway, my bag is too full. Once I'm at Beaudry, I sit in my usual spot near the station's entrance and text Jayden and Liam to tell them.

Jayden doesn't reply but bursts from the subway's staircase minutes later. He's wearing the shiny shorts from his cheerleading outfit over a pair of stretchy jeans. He says, "Wait, now I'm the one wearing a costume and you're not? What is this?"

"Oh, I have a costume. It's in my backpack. I'll put it on at the center. What are you supposed to be?"

Jayden unzips his jacket to reveal the rest of his cheerleading outfit.

"A cheerleader, duh! I felt it was a good way to introduce myself to the people at the Center. I've got the pompoms here. What are you gonna be?"

"I can't really tell you. It's coordinated with Liam's costume. You'd think I'm weird unless I show it to you."

"I already think you're weird."

"Noice. Hey, have I told you about my brother? He was in paper this morning, wait...."

I try to find a copy of today's *Metro* newspaper. It's usually distributed in subway stations, but it's after rush hour, and the paper box is empty. I need to look in the recycling bin to find a copy, folded in half.

"Eww, that's disgusting!"

"It's just the recycling, it's fine. Here."

I show him the page with my brother on it.

"Wait, that's your brother, really? Oh my God, what's up with your family?"

"Yeah, I forgot to mention it, he's fabulous too. What can I say, we have cool genes? Anyway, he's doing a drag show, and—"

"A drag show? At what, five?"

"He's ten! It's for a fundraiser for his scout winter camp. And he needs a costume, that's why I thought of you. Do you think you could lend him your old gymnastic leotard?"

"I see! Well, yeah, sure. I don't mind. As long as I get it back. It has sentimental value."

"Can you bring it tomorrow?"

"Of course."

We both sit down near the large window that looks onto Beaudry Street, where there's the feminist and LGBT+ bookstore. We stay like that in silence for a minute or two, until Jayden says, "'A scout drag show.' Your brother is outweirding you."

"Ha ha! He is."

"So, who're we waiting for? I've never talked to him."

"Liam. He said you have a couple of classes together."

"That's possible. I don't really pay attention. Cynthia's the one who knows everyone. Is that the guy who always wears the same hoodie?"

"He actually has several of the same type, in slightly different colors, but yeah, that's him."

"I had no clue he was gay. He sure doesn't look it."

What Jayden just said makes me feel awkward, but I try not to let it show. He really believes that you have to "look gay" to be part of the club?

"Well, I'm not sure if Liam identifies as 'gay....'"

"What is he, then? Bisexual? Or just, like, queer?"

"I'm not sure he'd be comfortable with us discussing his identity without him. You should ask him directly if you want to know."

"Ugh, fine. You're right. Sorry."

"It's all good. You'll see, he's great. Very easygoing. He draws super well."

"Oh, that's cool!"

"Yeah. Also, he's like a national swimming champion. He does international competitions and has won a bunch of awards. He's coming directly from his training, actually."

"Damn. Really? He looked more like a stoner to me."

"He's a bit of an introvert, I guess. He gets shy in large groups, but one on one, he's great, you'll see."

Soon after, Liam shows up, his hair wet as usual. We hug each other and I formally introduce him to Jayden. "Jayden, Liam. Liam, Jayden."

"Hi!"

They wave at each other. Jayden suddenly gets very excited. "Your hands! They're so tiny and cute, I love it. I know you're an athlete, so I would have thought your hands would've been strong and muscular, but no! Look at that."

Liam smiles awkwardly and puts his hands in the pockets of his black hoodie. Jayden probably sees a sign that his remark wasn't well-received, because he explains, "I meant that in a good way, of course. I like your hands. They look very delicate."

"Thank you. I'm also an illustrator, so having precise fingers help. But hey, we should go to the Center before they run out of food. I bet there's going to be more people than normal. They created an event on Facebook for Halloween!"

"You're on Facebook? That's for old people."

"You're *not* on Facebook? You're such a baby."

Oh no. They probably meant to be joking, but they both ended up sounding kinda mean to each other. I try to brighten the discussion. "So, Liam, you're still going to get moth makeup done?"

"Yes! If you're still dressing up as a lamp, of course."

"Hahaha! Wait, you're going as a lamp and a moth? That's so funny."

"Do you have a costume?"

Jayden reopens his jacket for Liam to see.

"I'll be a cheerleader. I know, very original."

"Well, it's not exactly a costume if you actually are a cheerleader."

"I'll get a zombie makeup done. Then I'll be an undead cheerleader."

"A zombie or an undead? They're not the same thing."

"Whatever, what's the difference?"

"A zombie is someone who was cursed by a shaman. Undeads are dead people who got brought back to life."

"You're such a nerd! I love it. But yeah, a zombie or an undead person, I don't care."

We all stop talking, although we still have an entire block to walk. I shouldn't have forced these two to spend time together, it was a mistake. I have serious regrets. Jayden says, "By the way, Liam, I wanted to know…. Are you, like, gay?"

Liam puts on his smug look that makes me melt, like he's about to get very petty. He tells Jayden, "That depends. Why are you asking?"

"Well, I just find it odd that you would go to a Halloween party at an LGBT+ Center, you know. Also, just by looking at you, we can't really guess, so…."

I facepalm internally. He should stop saying that kind of stuff.

"I don't know if I'm gay or not. Maybe, I don't know. I think I mostly like girls, but I make exceptions."

"So, you're a bit bisexual?"

"You could probably say that. But if I attend the LGBT+ Center's Youth meetings, it's mostly because I'm trans."

Jayden is in shock and stops. We were just steps away from the Center. Geez.

"What do you mean, you're trans? Like Alex trans? Or born in a girl's body trans?"

I interrupt him. "Oh my God, I'm sorry, Liam. Jayden,

you can't just scream that kind of stuff on the street. Maybe Liam doesn't want to talk about that."

"It's okay, I got this. I'm in good mood, but yeah, Alex is right, it's not something you can just ask people out of nowhere. I'm stealth at school, which means no one knows I'm trans. You can't tell anyone, it's between you and me. I don't have a 'girl's body;' my body is my own body, and since I'm a guy, it's a guy's body. But when I was born, people thought I would be a girl because of my genitalia."

"Seriously? That's so awesome. I really can't tell."

"You can't tell what? The shape of my genitalia?"

"That you're trans. It's pretty convincing."

"I'm not trying to convince you of anything. That's who I am."

"You know what I mean."

"I do and I wish you'd stop meaning that."

"I'm sorry. Besides Alex, you're the first one I've met who went through that."

"The first trans person that you know of."

Liam holds the door of the Center for Jayden and me. He says, "Don't worry about it. I know you mean well. I trust Alex's friends."

He winks at me as we walk inside. He's such a nice guy.

The Center is decorated in the spookiest dollar-store fashion. There's fake spider webs and purple garlands hanging from most surfaces and cartoonish cardboard ghosts on the walls. I show Jayden where he can put his jacket and take my costume out of my bag. In an instant, I'm draped in my silky bathrobe with the lampshade on my head. Jayden and Liam compliment me, and quite a few people passing by giggle at the sight. It was the easiest costume in the universe.

Nathan, dressed like the Joker from Batman, approaches us.

"Oh, there you are! I was wondering if you would come. I know Alex doesn't like partying that much. Excuse me, are you a lamp?"

"You guessed right!"

"But…why?"

"I'll be a moth," says Liam. "Our costumes are coordinated. A moth and a lamp. I'll go get my makeup done. Where is it happening?"

"Over there. She's very good." He touches his face. "She did this. But you don't need any makeup, you already look like a moth to me!"

Liam playfully sticks out his tongue to Nathan and goes in the direction our friend indicated. Jayden waves. "Hi! I'm Jayden. What's your name?"

Wow. Now, that was a skillful introduction. No wonder Jayden is so popular. I could never pull that off.

"My name is Nathan. I'm a regular, here. I live on the South Shore, an hour and a half away."

"Really?! That is so cool. I was on the South Shore a couple of months ago for the National Cheerleading Expo."

"You mean that isn't just a costume, you actually are a cheerleader?"

"In the flesh!"

Jayden and Nathan start chatting while I excuse myself to say hi to Armand, who is dressed as a vampire, and Mael-a, who's wearing a striped turtleneck and a beret (a French ghost? I don't know). They're preparing the buffet table. They inquire about how my week went and make some jokes about my costume (success!) before explaining what's on the menu tonight—compliments of India Palace, a curry house a couple of blocks away. There are different types of rice, lentil soup, naan bread, palak paneer, tikka masala tofu, and butter shrimp. Oh, and samosas, my favorite. The coordinator and volunteer shoo me away to finish setting up, so I go check on Liam, who's getting his face covered in gray and black makeup at a table in a corner. I say, "That will be beautiful."

"I'm going be the queen of the night. Just wait until you see the other parts of my costume!"

I go back to Jayden and Nathan to tell them about the food. I wouldn't want Jayden to think I'm leaving him by himself since we're on a "date," after all.

Nathan and I tell Jayden about all the activities at the Youth committee. We introduce him to a couple of the participants and staff, like Clementine and Sabrina, who were passing by.

Liam comes back with his face entirely covered in brown and grayish paint. He put on the rest of his costume, a white fluffy scarf that imitates the collar some moths have, and a cheap, black, plastic cape.

"Now, I can definitely see the moth in you."

"You're missing the antennas, though."

"Don't judge me, it's a last-minute costume! We decided to do it yesterday. And the cape is from when I went trick-or-treating as Batman four years ago."

"You keep all your Halloween costumes?"

I say, "You should see his house, there's piles of stuff everywhere! It's like a museum."

Liam adds, "More like an abandoned warehouse."

"Pose with Ciel. We need pictures."

Liam and I strike poses for Nathan's camera, and he promises to send them to us. I'm already thinking of making it my background image on my phone.

Jayden wants to go the makeup station, since he's supposed to be a zombie/undead cheerleader. But Armand gets everyone to be quiet, and announces, "Welcome to the annual LGBT+ Center's Youth Committee Halloween party! I'm Armand, the coordinator. I just wanted to tell you that the food is ready, so please serve yourself in a calm and civilized manner. We're going to have a short meeting here after the meal, and then show a spooky short movie in the chillax room. We'll tell you about it during the meeting. Until then, if you have any questions, feel free to ask me or our volunteer Mael-a. Enjoy the meal!"

Everyone gets in line for food, except Jayden. "Save me some! I'm not that hungry, so I'll do the makeup first."

When it's our turn, I just fill my plate with samosas. Liam notices and puts a spoonful of palak paneer on my plate.

"Hey! I don't want to eat that, Daddy. Samosas are fine."

"You can't just eat samosas. Palak paneer is spinach and cheese, you'll like it. Also, stop calling me Daddy."

"I will when you stop acting like you're my daddy!"

Nathan is laughing. He thinks Liam and I are hilarious.

The couch where we usually sit already being taken, we find a nice spot on the floor. The Center is very clean so no one complains. Jayden, now with black eyes and green cheeks, joins us while we're telling Nathan about our cycling trip last weekend.

"You should have seen it! It was like Liam's aunt knew me better than my dad. The cards were so on point!"

Jayden says, "You seriously believe in tarot? That's funny."

"I don't 'believe in tarot.' I'm just telling you it was mind-blowing."

"Do you like astrology, Jayden?" Liam asks.

"Not really. I think it's silly."

"What's your sign?"

"I'm not telling!"

Nathan laughs at Jayden's sassiness. Liam tries to get some information about Jayden's birth without any result. When I'm done eating, I get up. "I'm going to get some lamp makeup, be nice to each other!"

Liam tries to imitate my voice badly and says, "yes, Mommy!" but I play along and touch his forehead from above. "Especially you, you little brat!"

The person at the makeup station is named Pearl and often volunteers for the Center. I think she's a lesbian parent or something because I remember my dad talking to her at a Pride event under an LGBT+ family banner, and she was holding a baby.

"Hahaha! What are you supposed to be? A lamp?"

"Precisely! And I'd like lamp makeup, please."

With my consent, she covers the upper half of my face with a yellowish-white color, as if light was coming from the top of my head. Then, she paints a lightbulb on my forehead and a small chain from my scalp to my right cheek. When she's done, I put the shade back on my head and she hands me the mirror.

"You like it?"

"It's perfect, thanks!"

I hurry to get back to my group. Even from a distance, I can tell that Jayden and Liam are arguing, and not in a respectful exchange of ideas.

"It's not my fault if astrology is dumb. Just admit it's all fake."

"I'm not asking you to not find it fake or dumb, which by the way is a hurtful word for many reasons, I'm just asking you to respect that it matters to me."

"You should hear yourself talk! My God."

"That's enough! Both of you. We don't need to talk about it. Liam, stop asking Jayden for his sign or ascendant. He doesn't want to tell you. Jayden, respect that Liam is interested in astrology. That shouldn't be hard."

I sit between them because, apparently, I'm the biggest adult now. It's a good thing that the meeting is about to start.

Any attempt at having a discussion would have been met with knives in Liam's eyes and Jayden sharpening his teeth.

Everyone moves a bit to form some kind of circle. Mael-a and Armand formally introduce themselves with their pronouns (Armand uses "he" and Mael-a "they," like me) and invite us to do the same. They tell us we can also add something that was great about our week, something not so great, and what we like the most about Halloween.

Mael-a starts: "Something great: it's Halloween, which is my favorite holiday; something not so great: I didn't pass a math exam. What I like the most about Halloween is the costumes."

Someone who probably read my mind asks, "What are you dressed as? A French ghost?"

"No! Can't you guess?"

They put their gloved hands in the hair, against imaginary walls as if they were in a box and start making weird grimaces.

"A mime!"

"Exactly! Next."

One by one, we tell the group what we're supposed to say. Some people skip the "what was great and not so great" part and others hate Halloween (how?). Soon it's our turn. Liam goes first. "Hi, Liam here. I use he/his/him. Something great: I went on a cycling trip to visit my godmother with Alex." I smile and wave. He continues, "It was amazing. Something not so great: we have a bully situation at school. Oh, and huh, I guess I like Halloween because I'm an eternal emo at heart."

"That is true. Hi, I'm Alex, or Ciel. I use they/them/ their pronouns. Something that was great: I'd say the bicycle trip as well, it was really nice. Also, I kinda made up with my best friend? We had a fight, but now it's better. Something that wasn't so great…. One of my friend's friends leaked nude pictures of one of my classmates, and the entire school saw them. It's been really hard for a lot of people, but probably most for my one classmate."

"Ouch."

"Sorry to hear that."

I skip the Halloween part; I don't think I can come up with anything silly to say after that. Liam takes my hand. Someone asks, "Wait, are you dressed as a moth and a lamp?"

"We are!"

"Alright, cancel everything, these two won Halloween."

People giggle. It's Jayden's turn. "My name is Jayden, I use he and, uh, his. It's my first time coming here, so, hi folks. Something that was great: my cheerleading team performed our first full new set of the year, I absolutely loved it. Something that was not so great: I messed up several parts and even fell during the performance. I guess I'll do better next time. And why I like Halloween? The parties!"

"Hello everyone, I'm Nathan. I use he/his/him. Something that was great: my cousin made the finals of *The Big Quebec Dance-Off* and we had a big family party where I ended up coming out to my extended family."

The room bursts with congratulations and questions

about his cousin. Jayden has his eyes wide open. "You're kidding! I love *BQDO*. What's her name?"

"Salomé Tétreault. If you watch the show, vote for her!"

"Well duh, she's one of the best."

"Something that was not so great: one of my cousins got very sick at the party and my mom and I had to clean everything. Also, I like Halloween because chocolate is great."

Once every person has had their turn, Armand has some directives and closing statements for us, and we're free to wander around. Our little group stays on the floor, talking about the dance show Nathan's cousin is on, coming out stories (Jayden is seeking them, since he plans on coming out soon), and our love for chocolate.

At some point, Liam gets up and asks me, "Will you be alright getting home by yourself, Ciel? I'm not feeling too well."

"What? Sure. Will you be alright?"

"Yeah. I'm probably just tired from training. See you tomorrow at school."

Anyone can tell that he's upset, but he's already walking toward the exit. I get up as well and yell at him, "Wait! We haven't taken a Halloween selfie yet."

CHAPTER 14

I CAN TELL something is bothering Liam when I sit next to him in French, and he doesn't even offer to read my horoscope. He says hi and asks me how the evening ended, but it's more polite than interested.

"It was nice. We stayed a bit longer to watch some of the scary shorts they were showing, until Nathan had to leave for his bus to the South Shore. Then we stayed for one more movie and went home. Are you feeling any better?"

"Yeah. Yeah, I guess. I was mostly just tired."

We remain silent for a bit. The second bell rings and Ms. Campbell closes the door and tries to get people's attention, but everyone keeps talking. I tell Liam, "I'm sorry, I hope you didn't feel too left out."

"Don't worry about it, it's not your fault. I just don't really think Jayden and I get along, that's all."

"He can be quite self-centered...."

Ms. Campbell starts the lesson and Liam and I don't mention yesterday evening again. However, when class is over and Stephie and Leah catch us up in the hallway to ask us if we are still on for tonight's party, Liam shivers. "I'll pass, but thanks."

I feel bad, but he wasn't that interested in coming in the first place, since he wouldn't really know anyone there. I say, "I'll be there."

We agree to meet at the lockers at the end of the day and from there, go to Leah's house together and order pizza. We walk all the way to the staircase and chill a bit before the first bell, judging the costumes of the students who dressed up for Halloween. Leah gets very excited. "Have you seen that girl who literally dressed up as our school itself? She made some sort of model in cardboard and is wearing it as a jumper. It's hilarious!"

"Can't beat Liam's and my costumes from yesterday. Look at our selfie."

"That's so cool! Why didn't you guys dress up today?"

"Hey, I'm wearing my unicorn skin, that counts."

"It doesn't, you wear it every day."

"Because it's Halloween every day...in my heart."

As the legend foretold, the first bell rings. Leah and Stephie go down the stairs, and before leaving, Liam says, "Can you forward me that selfie? For my archives."

"Well, duh! Of course. See ya!"

I have music in second period. Viktor is back from his suspension, playing his clarinet like nothing happened. Has it already been two weeks since he got kicked out? Time passes so quickly with assholes out of the picture. When I look at him, my gut reaction is disgust before it gives way to anger because Raquel is still on a break from school. It might be for the best. I do not wish her to bump into him. Ever.

As one would expect, we talk about him at lunch. Caroline had a class with him in the morning and apparently he got roasted with questions from everyone. The teacher even had to intervene.

"Do you think he's getting what he deserves?" Cynthia asks.

Jayden says, "What? Getting admiration from guys and high fives from random people? If he got one thing out of it, it's two weeks' vacation and more school cred."

"You forget the investigation by the police, though. That's still going on. That's mostly what we were asking him about this morning. He was acting all tough, but I bet it's making him poop his pants."

I add, "Nothing funny about pooping your pants."

"Hey, you two went to the LGBT+ Center last night. How was it?"

Jayden gives the girls a summary. I'm glad he liked it. Maybe that will inspire him to come again next week. I wouldn't mind. Caroline asks, "Who's that Liam person? He's a student here? Why isn't he having lunch with us?"

Jayden replies, "You know what you are, Caroline? You're a fag hag. You want to be friends with every gay boy at school. You hoard them."

"I'm not hoarding them, it's more like, collecting the set. And it's not my fault if you're so much cuter than the other boys!"

"Can't argue with facts. But Liam isn't gay, he's transgender. He's in our English class. You know, the guy who always wear hoodies and never talks?"

"Oh yeah, I always thought he was a weirdo. In a good way!"

"We actually had an argument over astrology, can you believe it?"

"Hey, you're talking about my friend."

"Sorry, Alex. I know you two are close."

Jayden, trying to redeem himself, continues, "I thought your costumes were great. You might have won the costume contest today."

There's a costume contest at the end of lunch. It's happening in the cafeteria, but the way it works is that whoever gets the most applause wins, so it's basically a popularity contest and a lot of people with really great costumes are boycotting it.

"I don't think so. Liam and I aren't popular enough."

"What were you dressed up as?"

I show the group the selfie Liam and I took yesterday. Caroline inspects the picture. "He doesn't look like he was born a girl at all. Unless he's going in the other direction?"

I take my phone back and tell her, "You can't say that. That's rude."

"I'm just curious! What should I say, then?"

"What a good moth, what a pretty moth. I'm sure it likes lamps very much."

She sighs. "Liam makes a very good moth."

To my relief, the subject changes to this weekend's performance of the cheerleading squad. Jayden gets very excited and says, while touching my arm, "Will you come again? I promise it'll be better."

"It was already really good, seriously. But yeah, with pleasure."

Lunch is almost over when the familiar voice of Guy, the person in charge of cultural activities and afterschool programs, resonates through the cafeteria speakers to announce the beginning of the costume contest and invite all contestants to come up on an improvised stage. There are a dozen people, accompanied by cheering from the crowd. They're invited to quickly explain their costumes at the mic. Then, Guy invites people to clap as loudly as they can to select three finalists, from which the crowd will choose a big winner.

I don't recognize anyone I might know amongst the contestants, except Sullivan, dressed as Rick, the disgusting and abusive scientist from *Rick and Morty*. Fits him quite well, I must say. It's such a lazy costume, I can't believe anyone would even consider voting for that jerk: he only had to put on a gray wig, a lab coat, and brown pants, and slap some green makeup on his chin for people to recognize who he was. When asked to explain his costume, he loudly burps in the mic before yelling, "I'm student Riiiiick! Vote for me! *Burp.*"

WISH UPON A SATELLITE

You can tell Guy is not amused but tries to keep it together while the audience goes wild. Once everybody has their turn, Guy determines the finalists: Sullivan, of course; the girl who is dressed as our school, with her huge jumper made of cardboard boxes; and finally, a guy who looks like he's in final year with a very realistic zombie costume. They each get a prize, a $20 gift card for a local bookstore. The final round begins, and even though I know the girl dressed as our school should win, I have to concede that the audience is making twice as much noise for Sullivan, who is congratulated by Guy. He gets another gift card, $50 this time, to spend at the music shop and burps louder than ever to celebrate.

Lunch ends with everyone more jaded about how rigged the system is.

★ ★ ★

At the end of the day, Stephie and I are waiting at our locker for Samira and Leah to join us like we agreed when all of a sudden Liam storms out of nowhere. He gets very close to me and whispers, "I just got out of English. There's this girl, Caroline, who asked me if it's true that I'm trans."

I roll my eyes to the back of my head.

"Seriously? I'm so sorry, Liam. I feel like this is my fault. She's Jayden's best friend...."

"I can't believe it. I knew I shouldn't trust that guy."

"Do you want me to say something?"

"When she asked me, I simply said I wasn't. It felt terrible.

I hate lying about it. It makes me feel gross, like I'm ashamed to be trans or something. I'm not. I just don't want to deal with the transphobia. She asked me in the middle of the classroom, in front of everyone. I'm sure tons of people heard her. Enough to start rumors."

"I will tell her and Jayden to never mention it again."

"Please do."

I've never seen Liam so agitated. He's sweating and his eyes don't know where to rest. I open my arms and hug him.

"I'm so, so sorry. I don't know what to say."

We stay like that for a moment. When he moves out of my embrace, he takes a deep breath and puts his palm on his forehead before saying, "I'm tired. I'll just go home. Have fun at the party."

Stephie and I watch him walk away. I tell her, "Dammit. I really messed up. Do you think I should stay with him?"

"Can't say. I don't know him that well."

"Ugh. I think he was already angry at me because of yesterday. Now he won't talk to me ever again."

"What happened yesterday?"

I explain to her how Liam and Jayden seemed to hate each other's guts from the moment they first met, and how it just got worse from there.

"Then, at one point, Liam just left. Everyone could tell he was annoyed."

"Well, if he can't deal with you having other friends…."

Leah and Samira arrive with their jackets and schoolbags. Stephie and I grab our stuff and we're ready to go.

While we walk to the subway station, I decide to text Jayden while Leah overshares how excited she is about tonight. I don't have Caroline's number, so I just send a message to Jayden. I'm afraid he's going to read it and be annoyed or decide we shouldn't be friends because I'm so much trouble, so I figure it's best to sugarcoat it and give some context.

Hi Jayden! I hope your practice goes well. Liam just came to see me and apparently Caro asked him if he was trans in the middle of the class? He was pretty upset since he's not out at school. You probably understand that! I should have told Caro at lunch that Liam doesn't want people to know about him being trans, so it's kind of my fault.... Would you mind making sure she doesn't tell anyone? I don't have her number. Thanks!

This might be the longest text I ever sent. It's almost a letter. I should have written the date at the beginning and started with "Dear Mr. Jayden LeBlanc" and ended with "Distinguished regards, Alex Ciel Sousa."

We enter the subway. I try to listen to Leah, but all I can think about is Liam's distressed expression when he came to talk to me. I send him a text when we exit at Langelier station—the Green line is too deep underground to to get any service.

Hey Liam, sorry again for earlier. I know this won't make it better, but I texted Jayden to ask him to tell Caroline about not talking about you being trans to anyone. I hope you forgive me.

As soon as I press send, Stephie pulls my arm toward her, so I avoid walking into a metal post.

"Watch where you're going, kiddo! And put your phone down, we're here."

Leah's place reminds me of Stephie's mom's apartment. It's a well-lit apartment on the first floor of a semi-detached house. Only her older sister is there when we arrive. She says, "My mom works until five, and my dad is an elementary school teacher, so he basically never finishes work. We'll order pizza when my mom gets here. Until then, we can start a board game. We have like, twenty different ones."

"Or we could just relax. I'm so tired! I had PE last period, we're doing field hockey and I wasn't on the bench even once."

We take over the couches in Leah's living room while she tries to be the best hostess by offering us drinks. She even has a bowl of candy set up. She introduces us to Glockenspiel, her friendly calico cat, who I hang out with on the recliner chair. Samira pokes Stephie. "Hey girl, tell us the news! I saw you giggling with Frank in the hall this afternoon. What's that about?"

"Oh God, it's silly. You know how he learned to sew, right? Well, he'd been working on a skirt for me before we broke up, and he finished it, but he didn't want to bring it to school because we're not together anymore and it would have been weird."

"Such a sweetheart. I have to give him that, he's very attentive to detail."

"So, we agreed to see each other this weekend."

"Like a date?"

"No? Yes? Maybe, I don't know. He wanted to talk outside of school. I'm going to meet him after his soccer game and we'll go get milkshakes, that's all."

That's all? Sounds like a date to me. I don't say a word, but I know very well that Stephie and Frank were regulars at MooMoo's Milkshakes, to the point that Stephie called it "their" restaurant. Going back there with Frank basically means she's ready to pick up where they left off. That thought fills me with dread. If it ended up being that simple, why did the tarot cards make the situation seem so complex and nuanced, when I asked them about it last week? They could just have said, "no, look somewhere else."

I'm lost in my thoughts when Stephie pushes my leg with her feet. She asks me, "What about you? How is it going with Jayden?"

"You're talking like we're already a couple. We're not even dating."

"That's why I'm wondering! When will you ask him out?"

"I guess I should, eh? His friends are already shipping us. It's already a thing, even though it hasn't started yet."

Everyone in the room goes "aww," which scares Glockenspiel away. Stephie continues, "Didn't you go the

LGBT+ Center's Halloween party with him last night? That counts as a date."

"It didn't feel like one. There were too many people. And he's so likeable, he probably made more friends in one evening than I have in years at the Center. I was thinking of going to see him perform this weekend with the cheerleading squad."

"Wait, what? You're going to see the cheerleading squad perform at a game? What game?"

"I don't know. I hope it's not basketball, I almost fell asleep last time…. Why do you care?"

"Because you're probably going to watch a soccer game featuring my ex-boyfriend."

Can't I just pay attention, for once? It's like I never learn. I say, "Yes. That's it. It's a soccer game. I remember now. You're right."

"Do you want me to come? I can make sure you don't fall asleep!"

"Sure. It could be fun."

I wish I could tell her how I'm more excited to spend an afternoon with her than seeing Jayden perform, but it would be a bad idea right then. We just smile and kick each other's feet.

Leah's mom (Bernice? Beatrice? Berenice? Bernie? I didn't hear but now I'm too ashamed to ask) finally shows up and orders dinner as soon as we agree on what we want. I manage to convince the group to get Mediterranean veggies, my favorite, on one of the two pizzas. In exchange, I promise not to touch any of the meat one, which isn't much of a sacrifice for me.

We get to meet Leah's sister, who came out of her bedroom when she smelled the pizza, and her dad, who looks really nice. Once we've eaten, the kitchen table is cleared to make space for the board games Leah is so excited about. In the first one, you need to create railroads to connect major North American cities. The board even features Montréal, even though it's far in the upper right corner. I sit next to my new best friend, Glockenspiel, who's been sleeping on that chair for hours.

While Leah reminds everyone of the rules, I check my phone to see if Liam or Jayden has replied. No luck. The message I sent to Jayden has a "seen" mark next to it, but not Liam's. I put my phone on the table.

In the middle of the game—I'm comically behind everyone else, what a surprise—I get a new message. Samira stops her move to watch me. Stephie asks, "Who is it?"

"Oh no. You won't believe me. It's Gabriel."

Stephie starts laughing. Leah and Samira are confused.

"Gabriel? The guy who's always wearing his hat inside? What does he want?"

"To know how my evening is. He's been flirting with me for weeks."

"No way! He's super mean all the time."

"You should set him up as a joke, like in that movie. That would be funny."

"Like in *Carrie*? You know how *Carrie* ends? Very badly."

"Not *Carrie*. The one where that girl gets hit by a bus...."

While my friends are debating the fate Gabriel should suffer, I reply.

We're having a small Halloween party. You?

I instantly receive his response.

We're having a big Halloween party. I felt lonely. I was just thinking about you.

I don't know what to say to that. Does he even know how creepy that sounds? I just write,

Oh, cool.

Do you think we could see each other this weekend?

I read that last text out loud. Stephie and Leah are chanting "Fake date! Fake date!" while Samira says Gabriel could have demonic powers to retaliate against us.

"Alright, alright. I'll tell him I'm free on Saturday." I look and smile at Stephie in defiance. "I'll meet him at MooMoo's Milkshakes after the game."

"Yes! Good idea. Then I'll be able to watch if anything happens."

"And I'll get to see the skirt Frank made you before everyone else."

"Win-win!"

I text the plan to Gabriel, who replies,

I'd rather see you in private.

Everyone is curious, especially Stephie. "What's he saying?"

"He...he can't."

"Aww. That's too bad. Hey, are we gonna finish this game or no?"

I think for a moment, and then send a last text to Gabriel before putting my phone away.

I'm not sure when I'll be free. I'll let you know, is that alright?

CHAPTER 15

SATURDAY AT NOON, Stephie texts me that she's picking me up at my house in an hour so we can go to the soccer game together. In the meantime, I'm watching Virgil rehearse his dance for the fundraiser. Yesterday, at his cub meeting, they practiced what they would do onstage next week, and now he's more excited than ever. Maybe the amount of sugar he's been ingesting since Halloween has something to do with it.

"It's just going to be the greatest thing you've ever seen. Cold, hard facts. We sold every ticket! Can you imagine? We could have filled an entire auditorium, like the place we went to see the *Nutcracker*. Everybody wants to do it again someday, even Léo, who always finds everything boring. I'm not supposed to tell you but Noah and him, you don't know them but they're kind of annoying, they're gonna be cowgirls and dance to 'Man! I Feel like a Woman!' It's gonna be magical."

"Stop talking! You're supposed to be rehearsing."

"As always, you're the voice of reason, dearest sibling."

When Stephie shows up at the door, I'm already wearing my jean jacket and a white scarf. I don't bring anything else, other than my wallet and phone since I'm planning on coming back home right after the game, unless Jayden wants to hang out. I don't want to be a burden on Stephie when she has her date with Frank, and I have a book report to finish. Stephie objects. "You're only wearing this? It's cold outside."

I sigh and fetch a hat with a pixelated pattern from the coat rack. Virgil implores Stephie to stay and watch his dance moves, but I've seen them enough times. "She's going to see them next Friday with everyone else. We bought her a ticket, remember?"

Stephie adds, "I wouldn't miss that for anything."

"Sweet! I'm sure you'll love it."

We head outside to catch the bus. It really is getting chilly. The sky is covered in dense, dark gray clouds and the air is charged with humidity. While waiting at the bus stop, we hold hands to make them warmer. She probably used moisturizer, because I did, and her hands are as soft as mine. She says, "Do you think it would be a good idea to get back with Frank? Or am I being delusional?"

"Don't ask me! I think the best idea for you would be to date your best friend who also happens to be me, so I'm definitely biased."

Stephie takes it as a joke, and even if it wasn't, I can't help but laugh as well. Silly me.

We arrive at school. It's still strange for me to be there outside of regular school hours. There are parents and younger siblings, just like when I came to see the basketball game, but also a lot of students. The soccer team probably has more fans. As we get near the field, I hear someone calling my name behind me: it's Nathan. Nathan, from the Youth Committee of the LGBT+ Center. I stare at him in confusion while he opens his arms as if he was about to hug me.

"Alex! I'm so glad you came. Jayden told me you were the cheerleading squad's number one fan!"

"Nathan! What are you doing here? I thought you lived super far away."

"I do. Jayden invited me for a sleepover at his house yesterday. I figured I might as well come see him perform!"

This revelation hits me like a punch in the gut. I try to keep smiling and tell him, "Makes sense. You remember Stephie?"

"Of course! You're always talking about her. Can I sit with you folks? I don't know anyone here."

"Absolutely."

We try to pick a spot high up in the bleachers to get a good view. There are a lot more people than last time. I let Stephie do the talking, because I still need to process the fact that Nathan actually slept at Jayden's house. Even though I have a hard time believing it was just a slumber party, I try not to jump to conclusions, but Jayden's remark about me not "being his type" resonates in my head. Nathan is quite literally the exact opposite of me—twice my size, short black hair, strong arms, glasses. If that's Jayden's "type," no wonder nothing has ever happened between us. I won't even get a participation trophy.

As the game is about to start, I try to recollect every interaction I've seen between those two. They did seem to get along quickly, especially in contrast with Liam. Am I too oblivious? Did their flirting just go over my head? I must be really dense not to have seen it coming. Suddenly, me being at the game almost feels humiliating. How could I be so gullible as to think I stood a chance with Jayden? I have to remind myself that I am there as a friend of Jayden, Cynthia, and Caroline, and as moral support to Stephie. Coming to the game was the right thing to do.

Suddenly, people in the crowd start booing. The soccer players have just run onto the field. Without missing a beat, Stephie gets up from her seat and yells, "Don't let him play! Leave him on the bench!"

I look at her, surprised. She only has to say one name to make me jump to my feet as well. "Viktor."

I scan the team to find the brown-haired boy who destroyed a girl's life a couple of weeks ago, and he's right there, grinning as if nothing had happened. I had forgotten it all started because the pictures were shared among the soccer players. *These* soccer players. If Viktor isn't Charles Tremblay, the fake profile who sent the mass email with Raquel's nudes, then the culprit is on the team, and I think I'm speaking for a lot of people here when I say we won't forget that easily. There are a bunch of students standing up in the crowd, but also many parents. We all start chanting "Kick him out! Kick him out!"—a bittersweet pun on the fact that we're talking about a soccer team. Nathan, who probably doesn't even understand what's going on, still stands up in solidarity. He's a cool guy.

Music blasts from the speakers. I recognize the song the cheerleading squad was performing to last time. This time, though, no one from the squad is moving: instead, they stay in a corner and start chanting "Kick him out!" with the crowd, and we're louder than ever. The team's coach stands up and goes over to Viktor. He says something to him, and Viktor looks pissed before throwing his water bottle on the ground and rushing to the changing room, while showing the audience his middle finger. Some bearded man goes down the bleachers to speak to the coach, and I guess it's Viktor's dad or parent because he looks very angry. They argue until some other adults join the coach in trying to calm the man down, but he ends up storming out as well. At this point, though, there's too much action going on and it's hard to follow, and Nathan, beside me, has to yell to be heard. "What's going on?"

As the speakers go silent and people start sitting back down, I summarize the events of the past few weeks for him. Stephie sighs in relief. "I'm so glad he won't be playing."

"Yeah. There's at least a bit of justice in this world."

The same song that cut off a couple of minutes ago suddenly starts back on, and the cheerleading squad spread out over the playing zone while the audience claps and whistles. The improvised protest seems to have energized everyone. Even I can tell that the cheerleaders' moves are driven by more vigor than last time. The crowd is pleased, especially Nathan, who is unashamedly observing Jayden. I can't blame him; Jayden's totally killing it.

Once their routine is over, the cheer squad leaves to a roaring applause, giving space to the soccer team members, minus Viktor. They're playing against Sainte Kateri Tekakwitha, a secondary school from the complete opposite side of the borough. Apparently, we have a history of rivalry (according to Stephie, who heard it from Frank). The players take their place on the field. We spot Frank, who looks a bit lost, trying to find someone among the spectators. Stephie waves shyly at him, and he just smiles like nothing else matters in the world before getting into position.

That was so cute I almost didn't feel my heart getting stomped on for the second time before the game has even started.

★ ★ ★

I try my best to still have a good time. At the end, our school wins. We go down from the bleachers so that Stephie and Nathan can congratulate Frank and Jayden, and while everyone is busy and happy and overwhelmed, I say good-bye to my friends and get back home swiftly, despite the first snow trying to glue my feet to the sidewalk.

My dad is lying on the couch, reading a book, when I come in. Virgil isn't there. He's probably at João's house. Borki's napping on his cushion by the window, which is covered in frost. The place is quieter than ever. I consider finishing my book report once and for all, but it would just add to the awfulness of the day.

I turn my phone on and look at the message I sent to Liam yesterday. There's a read tag next to it, but still no reply. He probably didn't have anything to say about it, or he's just been too busy with swimming practice. Or maybe he's really angry at me. Who knows?

I open the message I got yesterday from Gabriel. I entertain the idea of accepting his invitation to meet with him in private. Could it really be worse than being alone and sad? I type "hey" and press send.

Hey, what's up?

He replies almost instantly.

Not much, you? Just playing PS4.

Sweet. Turns out I'm free this afternoon. Wanna come to my place?

I imagine how angry Stephie would be if she knew I was seeing this boy by myself. But a part of me doesn't care anymore. I just need reassurance that I'm not worthless and unlovable.

Yes. I'll be there in 30 minutes.

I get up and go to the living room. I ask my dad, "Is it okay if a friend from school comes over?"

"Of course. Just tell me in advance if they're staying for dinner. I'm making cannelloni. Do you know if they eat meat?"

"Not sure. I guess he does? I'll ask him."

I tidy my room. I make my bed. Every piece of clothing on the floor ends up in the laundry basket, even the ones I could have worn again. I line up my stuffed animals on the shelf above my bed. I never do that, but Stephie does it all the time, and I always think it's adorable. I don't have as many stuffed animals as she does, and the ones I have are pretty beaten up, but it does the trick. I think.

The bell rings, which startles Borki. I rush to the door before my dad has the time to get up. Gabriel is behind it, wiping the snow off his eternal Canadiens hat.

"Hello! You didn't have trouble finding the address?"

"It was easy."

I introduce Gabriel to my dad and tell him where to hang his jacket. In the meantime, Borki is investigating the newcomer by sniffing him.

"This is Borki. He's a good boy. He's the best boy!"

"I don't really like dogs."

"Are you allergic?"

"No, I just think they're annoying."

"Borki isn't annoying. But we'll keep him out if you want, don't worry."

"Thanks."

"Do you want to see the house?"

Gabriel shrugs. I decide to give him a quick tour in case he needs anything.

"So, this is the living room. That's where my computer is, over there, if we want to play a game or something. We're lucky, because my brother is usually on it, but he's away right now. So if you want to see the games we have, it's a good time."

I resist the urge to show him my favorite spot on the couch. It's probably very uninteresting and he already looks bored. I take him through the hall.

"These are pictures of my family, in Brazil. That's my brother, here…and a very bad picture of me, don't look at it. The washroom is over there."

"Let's just go to your bedroom."

"Alright."

I lead him to my room. He looks around a bit, while I sit on the bed. I watch as he looks at my things on display with what might be disdain. Everything he lays his eyes on seems to tarnish, like a reverse King Midas. His judgement makes me feel icky. I start to hope he doesn't notice how my stuffed animals are all lined up on the shelf. I wonder if he thinks I'm the most boring person ever. We don't even have a PS4. I clear my throat. "So, is there anything you want to do?"

"I don't know. What do you usually do?"

"You mean, with my friends? Well, we have Netflix…."

"Yeah, let's watch something."

"I'll get the laptop."

I leave him alone while I fetch my dad's computer in the dining room. When I come back, he's going through the little boxes on display on my dresser. I want to tell him where I got each of them, because they each have a special little story, but I'm afraid he won't care and will just find me annoying. And for some reason he still scares me and I want to make sure he's pleased, so I just set up our watching station on my bed, placing all my cushions and pillows in front of the laptop.

"There you go. Is there anything we need? Snacks? Are you hungry?"

"I'm fine for now. Maybe later."

I sit on the bed, and he joins me. I let him choose what we watch, some silly comedy from the United States, and I lay down on my stomach to see the screen better. He imitates me but ends up too close to me for it to be accidental. Our shoulders are touching.

After a moment of being immobile and watching the show, I feel his eyes on me, and when I glance at him, he smiles awkwardly under his cap. So, I guess this is happening. I smile back at him, and he slips his hand on my waist. Even though he's objectively terrible, the idea that I could actually be desired by someone fills me with so much relief that I could cry.

We stay like that for a long, long time without moving an inch. His hand is becoming warmer by the minute. Is he expecting me to make the next move? Or are we supposed to stay like that forever? After a couple of minutes spent staring at each other instead of the screen, he says, "I want to kiss you."

I wait a minute, expecting him to act on it, but nothing happens, he's just there, not knowing what to do. It's kind of cute. I remove his red hat from his head and see his scalp for the very first time. He has short, black hair that looks so soft, it almost makes him handsome. I brush his lips with mine and wait for the result. It makes him want more, so he leans in closer and gives me what he probably imagines to be a very manly kiss, but it's just rough and gooey. He grabs the back of my neck, so I feel his spiky hair with my palm. It's even softer than I imagined.

Once we're done exchanging saliva, we lay still for another moment. The movie keeps playing and we probably missed a huge part of it, but whatever: I didn't understand much of what was happening anyway because Gabriel insisted we watch it in English, and I'm not that good at it, but I was too ashamed to ask for subtitles.

He looks at me, his green eyes seem confused. I wonder how much he hates himself. He doesn't want to like me, and I don't want him to either, but here we are, smooching on my bed. It's absurd. I decide to at least make the most of it. I lift his left arm and place it on my right shoulder so I can nest on his torso. He doesn't seem to understand what I'm doing. I just smile to him, so he rolls with it and embraces me delicately. I want a tighter hug, but it still feels nicer than his damp attempt at French-kissing.

When the movie ends, he removes his arms from around me and sits on the edge of my bed. I get on my knees and rearrange my hair.

"My dad said you can stay for dinner if you want. He's making cannelloni. He just needs to know if you're a vegetarian."

"I'm a carnivore. And thanks, but I should go. This was nice."

We smile shyly at each other, and I let my head rest on his shoulder as a token of my appreciation. He says, "Just so we're clear, you can't tell anyone about this, get it?"

"Yeah. That's what we said."

He gets up and I go with him to the door. He puts his jacket on and says good-bye before disappearing into the snowstorm. I hear my dad's voice behind me. "I take it he won't stay for dinner?"

"Nope."

"He's a new friend of yours? I don't think I've seen him before."

"Kinda. Someone from school."

I sit on the couch, in my favorite spot, and play a bit on my phone before we hear the doorbell. My dad looks at me and I get up to see who's there. It's Gabriel, again.

"I think I left my cap in your bedroom."

CHAPTER 16

STEPHIE TEXTS ME a picture of the skirt Frank made her before the cannelloni is ready.

Since you wanted to be the first to see it….

It's a layered white skirt with an infinite amount of lace at the bottom of every panel. It's pretty, classy, and totally something Stephie would wear.

Darn, he's talented. Will you wear it to school on Monday?

I can't give him that satisfaction. I'll wait a week or two. Anyway, I was thinking that we should have matching outfits, you and I. It's been a while.

Sure. Stripes?

Meh. Floral patterns?

Black and white or colored?

Let's do black and white. How was your afternoon?

Relaxing. Just stayed home.

Lies! My kingdom is made of lies. What else should I do? Tell her that against her advice, I went and made out with this sad and creepy boy? She doesn't need to know. I'm afraid she would just pity me.

I don't ask her how her date went either. I suppose it was great, otherwise she wouldn't even consider wearing that skirt to school.

Virgil comes back, and we eat my dad's cannelloni. Gabriel won't know what he missed. I spend the rest of the evening trying to get through the graphic novel Liam lent me a couple of weeks ago that I never finished. Now, any reasonable person would tell me that I should focus on finishing my book report instead, since our next class is the ultimate extended due date, but what can I say? I have priorities and I love living dangerously.

On Sunday, I stay inside the whole day. It hasn't stopped snowing since I left the soccer game, the day before. I sit my butt down and get to work. I have to re-read Stephie's book report for like, the tenth time, because I forgot what the book was even about, but this time the words are flowing. Maybe

I'm freed by the fact that I don't have to care about any of my crushes anymore. It's like the absence of any expectation from life allows me to bullshit my way through the end of that book report once and for all. A nihilistic performance.

This is it. I'm done. It's over. I mean, the book report, of course. I start correcting my numerous mistakes—my new approach to life isn't as effective with spelling and grammar as it is with creating meaningless content, sadly—when I receive a text from Liam.

Can I call you?

This type of message has a tendency to make me panic. It must be serious if he needs to talk to me over the phone. Couldn't he just tell me what the call is going to be about? That would ease the stress. He never replied to the message I sent to him on Friday, so I guess it's about the whole situation with Cynthia and Caroline spreading the word about him being trans. I take a deep breath, since it promises to be emotionally draining, and type,

Of course, anytime.

A couple of seconds later, my phone rings. Sounding like someone who just got off a rollercoaster, and without saying hi, Liam's voice rains on me.

"Okay, so you absolutely won't believe me, but hear this out. Yesterday, my mom and I went to this birthday party for one of her friends, her name's Manon. She's also a painter but way more successful than her. I know my mom struggled for a bit because she must have been jealous, but at the end, friendship prevailed. Anyway, that's not important. While I was at my swimming practice, my mom made maple syrup baklavas for the party, I don't think she's ever made them while you've been here, which is a shame because they're so good. She placed them on our fancy crystal plate, and that bit is important, because it's a very peculiar dish. She sprinkled candied maple syrup and pistachios on the baklavas. When I saw it, I told her, 'You're so great with desserts! If only you cooked more often.' It was only teasing because she only cooks on special occasions. More often than not, I'm the one cooking for her."

"Yeah, I've seen it happen."

"So, we left for the subway, after she had wrapped the fancy crystal plate in cellophane. She had to carry it on her lap so I could help her with her wheelchair, because at that point, the snowstorm was getting pretty bad. We get to the station and when the train pulls up at the platform, we get in, of course. But then there was this couple standing in front of us and it seemed like they were having a good time. When they saw the baklavas, they were like, 'Oh, that's a lot! They look amazing. Will you need help with them? Are you gonna share?' Blah blah blah, you know, usual random stranger banter. My mom and I were like 'ha ha ha,' laughing politely before ignoring them. We get off at Préfontaine station, arrive at the party. Don't get any ideas, it was an old people party, besides me there was only one kid, a five-year-old who ended up falling asleep right after we ate."

"I'm surprised that wasn't you!"

"Yeah, same. I could've used a nap. Anyway, the baklavas were a hit. None were left, and I suspect Patrick, some writer who came to our house a couple of times, went as far as licking the crystal plate, he liked them so much. We finally leave, and it's still snowing pretty badly, so I help my mom with her wheelchair again while she holds the crystal plate. We arrive at Préfontaine, miss the train by a couple of seconds, and it was kinda late in the evening, so trains were like every ten or fifteen minutes. It finally arrives, the door opens, we get inside, and bam! Who's right in front of us?"

"That cheesy couple?"

"Yeah! What were the odds? I still can't believe it. They looked a lot more tired than earlier, and this time they just stared at us in shock, and I don't blame them. The guy said, 'Uuuh, how was the dessert?' and we just couldn't help but laugh all the way to Langelier, where we got off."

"That's an insane coincidence."

"Wait, listen to this. So, you know there's a library right by the pool where I have my swimming practices? It's a small branch, and for the kids and youth sections, you have to return the books directly to the librarian for him to scan them in. Before my practice this afternoon, I decided to return some books that were overdue, and I was only half paying attention because I was running a bit late, and the librarian just said, 'You have a balance of two dollars and fifteen cents, but I'll cancel it for one of these baklavas.'"

"Wait, was it the same guy?"

"It was the same guy!"

"Whoa."

"I know!! I told my mom about it, and we'll definitely bring him a baklava at some point."

"Look at you, bribing the librarian for a two-dollar fee."

"It'll be hilarious."

"And dangerous with all the books. Maple syrup is sticky."

Liam giggles diabolically before adding, in a suddenly serious voice, "I wonder what it means."

"What what means?"

"These encounters. These patterns."

"I don't think it means anything."

"What if I want them to mean something?"

"It only means that the world is small."

"It's not small. There's like, three million people in Montréal."

"Three million? For real? That's a lot."

"That's what I'm saying."

"Let me check."

I do a quick search on my phone and come back to him. "Montréal itself is only one-point-seven million. The greater Montréal area is four million."

"Well, one-point-seven million is still huge! That's the population of a small European country."

"I guess."

I feel like we've covered this subject thoroughly, and I swear to myself it's the last time I doubt his knowledge of

geography. I wait for a short moment before asking, "So…
are we still friends?"

"Of course we are. You're such a potato."

"I don't know! You never replied to me. I was getting
nervous about it."

"I'm still upset about the whole situation at school, but
it's not the end of the world. I'll see how it goes. Hopefully,
you were convincing enough that no one else will hear about
it."

"It should be alright. They're not transphobes, you know.
They're my friends."

"I know. I'm just in a bad place right now."

"What do you mean?"

"Well…. Depression, and stuff. I told my coach yesterday
that I'm considering quitting the team after Christmas."

"Really? That's huge. Are you sure?"

"I don't know. Maybe? That's why it felt weird to see that
guy in the library this morning. It's like the universe is trying
to tell me something."

A heavy silence. I ramble, "Maybe…it's telling you to…
trust the people…who are, you know, recurrent in your life.
Like me, or other classmates…."

He laughs. "Maybe it means I'm stuck with them in my
life, is that it?"

"Yeah, so you shouldn't be angry at them, that would
be bad."

"I guess you're right."

Then that's settled. We're still friends. Every one of the muscles in my body relaxes. I tell Liam, "I went to the soccer game at school yesterday, to see Jayden cheer. You know Viktor is on the team? Or was, I'm not sure. The crowd almost rioted because he was about to play. We were chanting 'Kick him out! Kick him out!'"

"Hahaha. 'Kick him out.' At a soccer game."

"I'm glad you appreciate the pun. People were so angry!"

"I bet. Did it go well with Jayden?"

"Not really, and I don't think it will ever go anywhere. He's dating this guy, now."

"Oh no! Sorry to hear that."

"It's okay. I don't think he's ever been anything more than a crush to me."

"I'm glad you see it like that."

We stop talking again, but this time it's even more awkward because we're both kind of sad. I can't help but think about how we should just get together, him and I. Why does it seem so obvious to me but not to him? What a tragedy. I say, "Well, I'll see you tomorrow in French."

"Yeah. Are you done with your book report yet?"

"I would be if you'd stop interrupting me to talk about your baklava adventures."

"'My baklava adventures.' I love it. I'll leave you alone, then! See you tomorrow."

★ ★ ★

Stephie and I meet at the lockers in the morning, and before saying anything we look at each other in delight: she went for a classy grunge look, wearing a dark-blue, jersey dress to match her medieval-looking floral tights, while I went full 2010 with shorts-over-leggings and a floral printed vest and tie. We're wearing the fancy lip gloss that we both have. She winks and says, "Sexy!"

So, I rest my head against the locker and say, with a deep and awkward voice that was meant to be sensual, but ended up just sounding corny, "Want a piece of it?"

She pushes me and we giggle before getting our stuff for French class. I show her my book report. She holds it high up in the air and says, as if she was having a revelation, "The oracles have spoken true! You really did write it...." She flips through the three pages. "And it's almost not entirely false!"

When we arrive in class, we split up and I place my assignment on Ms. Campeau's desk. On a scale of one to ten, where one is not that much of a relief and ten is the biggest relief ever, handing in my book report is a solid eleven. It's a liberation. It's alleviating, as Liam says about swimming. Not having to care about boring mandatory stuff sure feels great. I wouldn't be surprised if it was one of the reasons why Stephie always hands in her assignments first. I'm sure it gets addictive.

Liam isn't there yet, but I sit at our table and, while waiting, I start debating if I should have lunch with the cheerleading squad or not, considering how they handled the information that Liam is trans. I'm also kind of bothered by how quickly Nathan and Jayden got together, while in my mind, we flirted for weeks without anything happening. I'm not annoyed at him, but the whole thing makes me feel undesired and it's a yucky thought.

Luckily, Liam shows up with the daily newspaper and honors his tradition of reading my weekly horoscope, which provides good insight to my dilemma. "Tensions will be eased today, so don't hesitate to cut through the weirdness and move on."

I settle on having lunch with the squad. I'll switch back to sit with Stephie and her friends by the end of the week.

At noon, Liam and I walk to my locker together so I can give him back his graphic novel.

"Did you like it?"

"You bet! It was great. Loved the ending."

"See? Reading can be fun!"

"Stop it, you sound like a first-grade teacher."

He leaves for his house while I grab my lunchbox. On my way to the cafeteria, I see a familiar hat in the middle of the flow of people. It's Gabriel, walking by himself in the opposite direction. I position myself so that we have no choice but to bump into each other. When he passes nearby, I wave at him. He raises his head, so the visor of his hat isn't blocking his view. His eyes cross mine. I say, "Hey."

He smirks but doesn't say anything and keeps walking.

A smirk.

I guess that's better than nothing.

At the lunch table, as one would expect, Jayden and Caroline are talking about their Saturday performance. Cynthia is still in line for the cafeteria meal. I join them just in time to discuss the spontaneous protest against Viktor that erupted before the game. Cynthia says, "I'm really glad it happened. I was feeling sick to my stomach at the idea of having to cheer for him."

I add, "It honestly felt so good, yelling to kick him out. I had no clue I needed to do that so badly."

"I'm not even slightly sorry for him. You saw how he raised his finger to everyone?"

"What a jerk."

Cynthia arrives with her meal tray. "You're still talking about Viktor? I'm so tired of hearing about him."

"Yeah, let's talk about someone else. I saw you changed your relationship status on Facebook, Jay-Jay!"

Jayden can't help but show a large smile. He finishes his bite and explains, "It's that boy you saw after the game."

"That tall, dark-haired guy? Oh my God, I thought he was hot."

"His name is Nathan. We spent the weekend hanging out together. Yesterday, he asked me if I wanted to be his boyfriend, so now we're officially dating."

"How could you keep that from me, Jayden LeBlanc?"

"It literally only happened fourteen hours ago, at the bus station at the end of the Green line! It was almost midnight when I got back home. I was so tired, I figured I'd tell you today."

"I'll never forgive you."

"Yeah, yeah. Anyway, we're trying something. He lives two-and-a-half hours away, on the South Shore. Oh, but Alex, you'll love this—turns out I won't have to come out to my parents!"

"What happened?"

"You're going to laugh. It was yesterday evening before we left for the bus station. We were just talking on my bed, and he asked if he could kiss me, so we kissed, and then we just kept kissing. My mom opened my door to ask us what we wanted for dinner, right at the wrong moment. You should have seen her face! She didn't even finish her sentence; she simply closed the door. It was like 'Hey boys, what do you want for diiiiinnnnneeeerrr?'—slam!"

"I can totally imagine Maggie doing that."

"The sweetest part is when she came back. She knocked, that time, like she's supposed to. I told her she could come in. She said: 'I just wanted you to know that we're totally fine with it,' something like that. 'And Nathan, you're always welcome here.'"

"Aww!"

"Then she left. And then…SHE CAME BACK! She needed to know what we wanted for dinner."

"Hahaha. That's precious! I love your mom."

That's a nice story. It's cute. But as I sit there just listening to it, I can't help but wish it had been me in Nathan's place. Maybe not kissing Jayden, that would have been weird. But

I did want to be helpful to him. I was supposed to help him come out. Now it just happened by itself. How useless can I get?

Caroline says, "So when are you going to see him next?"

"Wednesday. He usually goes to the weekly youth gatherings at the LGBT+ Center. That's how we met, thanks to Alex! Will you be coming this time?"

Everybody turns toward me, and I don't know what to say. I could technically go, but I don't feel like playing the third wheel with a couple who will probably spend the whole time being all touchy-feely.

"Actually, I need to check with Liam. That's usually our evening out. It'll depend on if he wants to go."

"Is he still angry at us?"

"He's not angry at anyone. He's not the kind of guy to hold a grudge against people. He's just scared that the entire school might end up knowing he's trans, which I totally get."

Cynthia says, "I'm so sorry about the whole thing. I shouldn't have said anything to Melissa. She's the one who asked her if it was true."

"Him."

"What? Oh, right, sorry. I need to get used to that."

I raise my eyebrow. Get used to that? It had never been a problem until she learned he was trans.

But I don't have time to say anything because a roaring *gasp* crosses the cafeteria, and a wave of students swarm to the side of the room. There are shouts and screams. In the confusion, Andrea, one of the older cheerleaders, jumps on our table to get a better look at the scene. "It's that kid who got kicked out of the soccer game, Saturday. Now, he's getting a proper beating!"

Jayden, Cynthia, Caroline, and I run toward the mass of people, trying to get a glimpse of the action. I can't see anything, and people are pushing, so I stay on the side, but I clearly hear the two names the crowd is loudly whispering: Viktor and Frank.

CHAPTER 17

ON WEDNESDAY, I have a Science and Technology class, and it feels so weird to arrive and see Viktor in his usual seat without Frank at his side. He's been suspended for the week. It's like the two of them are playing musical chairs. The most absurd rumors have started about their fight on Monday. Some said that Frank was the one who sent the emails and Viktor was about to tell the police about it, and that he was only protecting himself. Others think he wanted to avenge Raquel. Some people are making a martyr out of him. Stephie called me the other night and she told me the truth, which isn't as clear as people are making it out to be. It's actually much more nuanced. She said, "During our date at MooMoo's Milkshakes, I told him that if we were to date again, I didn't want to have anything to do with Viktor."

WISH UPON A SATELLITE

"That's why he punched him? To prove something to you?"

"No! That would be worse. Having boys punch each other for my love…. Ew! Frank isn't that kind of guy. And I don't want him to be."

"Then what happened?"

"At lunch, he told Viktor he wasn't welcome at their table anymore. That made Viktor upset. He said he would tell the police that it was Frank who sent the email. Which is a lie. Frank replied that everyone on the team knew he sent it himself."

"Wait, is that true?"

"Frank isn't sure, but that's what he thinks. After that, Viktor apparently said he would tell the whole school that…," she paused, then whispered, "that his girlfriend has a dick."

"Oh, fuck that guy. Well, not literally, he doesn't deserve it. I'm sorry to hear that. What a coward. Weaponizing your transness against Frank. I can't believe we used to consider Viktor a friend. How insecure must he be!"

"Yeah. And I'm not even Frank's girlfriend anymore. But anyway, that's what made Frank punch him. Obviously, you can't tell anyone."

Then I asked her if she was going to take him back after that. She said the fact that he beat up this macho turd wouldn't make up for everything else, but that considering the circumstances, it wouldn't be an argument against it, either. Which is understandable.

From my seat near the front of the classroom, I glance over my shoulder to look at Viktor. Frank really didn't miss.

The corner of his right eye is bruised, and a lip injury is still healing. I wonder who could pity him. Then an annoying laugh comes from the back of the classroom. I know who it was: Sullivan. Who wants to bet that when Frank gets back from his expulsion, Viktor will have a VIP seat waiting for him with the cool guys? They're all made of the same dirt, composted from their rotting egos that don't know how to feel alive without diminishing others.

I'm not sure if it's the knowledge of having nothing to lose, recklessness, disgust at their hypocrisy, or all these things at once that makes me do it, but before class starts, I get up. I walk with a surprising amount of confidence to Gabriel's desk, and I sit on top of it. I smile at him while he looks flustered.

"What do you want?"

"Nothing. Just to say hi."

All the boys turn toward me with confusion. I add, flirting with Gabriel, "How are you today?"

"None of your business. Go away."

"Hey, no need to be rough. I was just asking."

I slide down from his desk. I know better than to use Gabriel's sexuality to humiliate him, but I feel the need to poke at the wound and remind him that it's still right there, as the entire world is burning. "I'm saying this not as a friend, but as your sibling. You should really know better. And please, try to get your shit together. I'm not here for you to play with and dispose of whenever you feel like. Am I being clear?"

He doesn't answer. The bell rings and I hear Mr. Brazeau's voice saying, "Alex, would you mind getting back to your seat so that everyone can have the time of their lives exploring the magical world of electric circuits?"

And as I walk back to my chair next to Jayden, Sullivan says, full of disdain, "What was that?" Nothing from Gabriel.

I didn't know such a feeling of bliss could exist.

★ ★ ★

Stephie arrives early at my house on Friday afternoon so we can get ready for Virgil's drag talent show together. I recognize the dress she's wearing. We bought it together ages ago when she made a ton of money babysitting. It's light pink with a Peter Pan collar and a small belt. I suddenly feel very boring with my suspenders and jeans, so I tell her to entertain my brother while I go change into something less casual, which ends up being a yellow, polka-dot, crinoline dress, as if we were going out dancing.

When I come back to the living room, Stephie is doing Virgil's makeup, something flashy and sparkly to go with Jayden's old gymnastics leotard, which he's wearing with bright pink legwarmers. When my dad comes to see if we're ready to go, he can't help but laugh. "My eyes! My eyes are melting. This is so beautiful."

We take pictures before getting dressed to go outside. The sky has been clear all day, and the afternoon sun has melted some of the snow, but the weather is still as cold as the rest of the week. We have to be careful because the sidewalks are slippery.

We arrive at the church basement where Virgil has his cub meetings. After my dad gave the tickets to the person at the entrance, which my brother recognized as "Baloo," we get to the removable stage that's been set up for the show. We follow Virgil behind a black curtain, where all the kids are. It feels like we're at an anime convention, but even more camp—everyone has colorful and ridiculous outfits, probably borrowed from other people for most of them, because they all look so exhilarated to be able to dress like that in public. They're busy teaching each other how to walk in heels. One of them is even wearing huge, sparkly, disco platform shoes. I wonder where they even found those. There's an adult drag queen running a makeup station in a corner.

We bump into Virgil's best friend, João, dressed as a white rose. His head is coming out of the petals and a big felt bee springs from his white hat, an image I never knew I needed to see until now. I take my phone out. "Both of you, strike a pose! We'll put that on Dolores von Tragic's Instagram."

João steps out to get his backpack. "Wait, I need my sunglasses."

He pulls a pair of huge, flower-shaped sunglasses out of his bag and places them on his nose, and he and my brother make the most terrible duck faces they can for my camera. Once I get a good shot, my dad, Stephie, and I leave them to join the rest of the spectators on the other side of the curtain.

The entire room is now filled with people, and I'm glad parents and siblings have a special section reserved for them, because otherwise I'm not sure there would have been seats left for us. My dad sees João's parents and starts chatting with them in Portuguese, and even though I understand most of the words, I can't really follow what they're saying. Stephie and I claim seats in the second row. She subtly points at a pair of parents in front of us who look so confused and whispers, "Do you think they're afraid of their poor little boy catching the genders?"

I can't help but laugh uncontrollably. They do seem like they don't get what's happening around them at all. The man is holding onto a bottle of water and taking nervous little sips.

Around us, other parents appear genuinely happy to be there and excited about the show. Stephie spends time judging people's outfits until the lights go down a little and everybody sits down, including my dad, who's still talking with João's parents, two rows behind us. Apparently, that's where he's going to sit. He probably wants to give Stephie and me some privacy.

Stephie giggles with excitement when the room turns completely dark, and I think this is the most endearing thing she's ever done. The opening act kicks off, and an overstimulated miniature Ariana Grande lip-syncs and dances to a pop song. That kid is exhibiting way too much energy. It's worrying, vaguely artistic, and definitely entertaining. When the song ends, we all clap and cheer, and someone wearing a cub uniform but with a skirt, pigtails, and exaggerated makeup comes to the microphone to announce, "Thank you misses, misters, and everyone else, for being here with us tonight! Now please join me in welcoming our hostess and mysterious canned fish tycoon, Dolores von Tragic!"

"The Eye of The Tiger" starts playing and my brother dramatically steps onstage to thunderous applause. The music fades. In her most ridiculous voice, Dolores von Tragic says, "Yes, keep clapping, my dears, keep clapping, for tonight, we are all gathered to help raise funds for, uh…." She looks for a paper in the pocket of her vest and frowns. "'A magical winter camp for the Montréal cub scout section 529?' What the heck? Oh well, whatever."

(The audience laughs.)

"My name is Dolores von Tragic, heir to the von Tragic canned tuna empire, and I will guide you through this delightful evening. And without further ado, please welcome to the stage the amazing Deborah Debourg!"

This time, when we're done cheering, Stephie smiles at me emphatically and takes my hand. Neither of us expected to have this much fun, and now it feels like a date, and suddenly there's no other place I want to be in this world other than on these uncomfortable, church-basement plastic chairs.

Deborah Debourg arrives onstage. She swipes the audience with attitude, before a karaoke version of "L'amour est un oiseau rebelle" from the *Carmen* opera starts playing. To everyone's surprise, she sings for real, with a textured falsetto voice and with rolled Rs as if we were in nineteenth-century France. But even though the skills are impressive, I can't detach my mind from the warmth of Stephie's hand. It purifies me, just like that kiss we shared, and her lips feel so close and so far at the same time. What's up with her? She exudes love.

When that child prodigy is done, Dolores von Tragic

introduces a duo of cowgirls, performing a silly dance to "Man! I Feel like a Woman!" It's painful to watch, but they seem like they are having a good time, so there's always that. I remember Virgil said they were the annoying kids, so I hope getting to express themselves will do them some good.

At that moment, my thoughts get polluted with the image of Gabriel. I can't believe I let him touch me. Am I that weak? Did I need attention so badly that I would hide the things we did from Stephie? It feels like a betrayal. I lied to her, and for what, exactly? I was only trying to relive some of the things she made me feel, but by trading her for this poor excuse for a lover.

After the cowgirls, a tiny kid in a big, puffy, blue dress and a white braided wig is invited on the stage. She doesn't say anything but pulls a recorder from inside her dress majestically, and starts playing "Let it Go" from the movie *Frozen*. From her facial expressions, we can tell this isn't supposed to be good, and the crowd, Stephie and me included, appreciates the humor and laughs.

What I don't get is how I'm supposed to differentiate between friendship, love, and desire. They're all kind of the same to me. Maybe I only say that because I only have a few close friends, but I have the tendency to develop crushes on every one of them. Maybe it's because we're rare or invisible. That would explain why I need to keep them so close to me.

What I see on the stage right now makes me believe that perhaps we're not so rare. How many of us are holding it all inside, waiting for the moment when it feels safe to be ourselves?

That's so cheesy, but take these three kids, who come onstage after the Disney ice queen is done murdering our ears with her recorder (she was awesome, by the way). They're wearing beautiful, long, jazz dresses and heels, and are singing an a cappella version of "Like a Prayer" by Madonna, with one of them beatboxing. They look like they're having the time of their lives.

The acts succeed one another. There's more lip-sync of Adele and Céline Dion (João does a wonderful impression of the diva), a heartfelt acoustic guitar rendition of "How Far I'll Go" from the movie *Moana* (which moves parents to tears even though the musician was wearing the most atrocious makeup of the evening), and finally, Dolores von Tragic's closing act, where she sings and dances to "It's Raining Men." Then, all the kids come back onstage for a final bow, and the scout leader, Bagheera, wearing sparkly leggings and an iridescent vest (a beautiful contrast with his beard) takes the mic to say a few words. "I must say that when Ms. Dolores von Tragic approached me with her idea of a drag talent show, I was skeptical, but wow! Have you seen this? That was amazing! They deserve another round of applause. Also, let's hear it for our emcee, Virgil, A.K.A. Dolores von Tragic!"

As soon as he says my brother's name, Stephie and I let go of each other's hand and get up from our seats. The room bursts in applause. Someone (is it my dad? I can't tell, everyone is standing) throws a bouquet of flowers onstage, and the whole scene is just so perfect.

Stephie says, "I could deal with a weekly dose of that on Netflix."

"Wouldn't that be awesome?"

All the parents are trying to find their kids to congratulate them. Even the couple that seemed dubious at the beginning looks impressed. I manage to locate my dad in the chaos. He's with Virgil, but it's impossible to reach them because every adult wants to shake my brother's hand and every kid wants a selfie with him. Stephie says, "It might take a while. Should we wait for them?"

"Let me ask."

I text my dad to ask him if we can go ahead. Once we have his permission, we put on our hats and jackets and head out.

★ ★ ★

It's still early in the evening, but because of daylight saving time, the sun is already gone and the little snow that melted during the afternoon has now turned into ice. Stephie takes my hand, and we let ourselves slide on the sidewalk.

"Do you think they've installed the skating rink in the park, yet? They usually decorate the little house next to it at the same time."

"It might be too early. The snow is probably going to be gone by next week."

"You're so pessimistic."

"Excuse me, that's actually optimism. I don't really like the snow. It's cold."

"Oh, my poor child! Let's go see. It'll be pretty."

We cross the street and find an entrance to the Maisonneuve Park. Last time I was there was with Liam, a couple of weeks ago, but it's a completely different experience when there's snow: the bike paths are now used for walking, and there's cross-country skiing trails all over the place. I usually like to cut through the grass, especially to get where the skating rink is, on the opposite side of the park from where I live, but with the new snow and ice, we just follow the trail.

I'm feeling mellow, and I let Stephie do most of the talking. "What was your favorite act? I really liked that jazz trio; they weren't always on pitch, but it was such a sweet idea. I liked their energy. Also, they can walk in heels much better than I ever will."

"The opera singer was the most talented."

"Without a doubt. Yeah, I really liked that as well, although she had less of a presence onstage, you know what I mean? She went to the mic and didn't move. But I think we can agree that the best moment was with that kid who played 'Let it Go' badly on the recorder."

"It was torture!"

"Hahaha!"

We get to where the skating rink would be if it had been installed. There's nothing yet. And no trace of decoration on that little house where they serve hot chocolate and coffee during the day. Stephie says, "Oh well. It's still nice out."

"Yeah…."

We sit on a bench nearby and we look at the stars for a moment. Then she turns toward me and locks her eyes on mine. "Are you alright? You seem so sad."

I shrug. She says, "That's a no."

"I need to tell you something. Something that happened last week, after the soccer game. When I went home, I told Gabriel that he could come to my house."

"Why would you do that?"

"Because of everything. Liam was angry at me. Jayden started dating Nathan. You're getting back with Frank. I just felt gross and disgusting, like no one would ever be interested in me. I felt sick. So yeah, I told him he could come over. We cuddled. It was the most disgusting kiss ever. And then the next day at school, he just ignored me."

"I'm so sorry, sweetie. Don't take it personally. That boy is a loser."

I laugh as I wipe some tears that are turning into ice on my cheeks. "You bet he is. In science class, I went to talk to him in front of his friends, to tell him to get his shit together. That felt amazing."

"I would have paid to see that."

"I'm sorry, Stephie. I'm so sorry."

She leans even closer to me and squeezes my hand.

"You're sorry for what? For not telling me? That's silly. It's okay. I understand."

"No…. I'm sorry because I think I'm in love with you."

She looks at me with all the softness in the world.

"I know. It's complicated."

I lay my head against her shoulder and cry while she holds me until the stars stop shining.

ABOUT THE AUTHOR

SOPHIE LABELLE is an internationally renowned visual artist and author from the South Shore of Montréal, in French Canada. She is the transgender cartoonist behind *Assigned Male*, a webcomic about a group of queer and trans teenagers that has been running since 2014 and has already touched millions of readers.